The Drugstore

ALSO BY SD SHELTON

Me, the Crazy Woman, and Breast Cancer

The
Drugstore

A NOVEL

by

SD Shelton

ENLIGHTEN PRESS
A DIVISION OF ENLIGHTEN COMMUNICATIONS, INC.

Enlighten Press
A Division of Enlighten Communications, Inc.
Norman, Oklahoma

The Drugstore
Series Book One

First Enlighten Press trade paperback edition August 2017

Cover Design by Elizabeth B. Wren

Manufactured in the United States of America

10 9 8 7 6 5 4 3 2 1

Paperback ISBN 978-0-9825085-2-7
EBook ISBN 978-0-9825085-3-4

Library of Congress Control Number: 2017950438

For more information about special discounts for bulk purchases, please contact Enlighten Press at enlightenpress@cox.net

In Memory of my Grandparents

"I believe that we are here for each other, not against each other. Everything comes from an understanding that you are a gift in my life - whoever you are, whatever our differences."
- John Denver

Chapter One

Old Pete

The old glass door of the drugstore swung open, and the wind carried in with it a dry, brown leaf and a discarded gum wrapper. Fifteen-year-old Olivia Stephens, or Livy as she was known to her friends, was unable to see over the small jewelry counter. Only moments before, she planted herself on the thick burgundy carpet that ran the length of it.

Livy worked most Saturdays, and weekday afternoons when she got out of school. This morning, she had been dressing herself in an assortment of cheap baubles, the kind which eventually turned the skin green.

Livy hadn't yet arisen before she heard the slow shuffling steps from a pair of tan and well-worn moccasins. Scratch... scratch... scratch. The footsteps sounded like sandpaper. Livy knew immediately that it was Old Pete.

Old Pete was the town's oldest inhabitant and a Cherokee Indian. He wore moccasins and had a face as old as the earth. It carried in it the lines of a life wrought with hardship.

Old Pete wore a long black trench coat, even in the summer. His ebony and graying hair hung almost to his waist in two long braids. The dusty moccasins peeked out from the bottom of his coat with every slow and agonizing step he took.

The ancient man had been around as long as anyone could remember, but no one knew his last name or where he lived. However, all the merchants on Main Street knew where he would be every morning. The exception, of course, being Sundays when most of the little town's stores were closed.

Old Pete was like clockwork. At 8:30 a.m., he would make his first stop of the day at Harvey's Gas Station. The station sat where Main Street came to an end. A driver's only alternative was to leave town. Otherwise, they would need to make a U-turn around a circle median and return from whence they came.

Old Pete's ritual included him shuffling into the men's room and emerging fifteen minutes later, looking exactly as he had when he had gone inside. Next, he traveled up the west side of the street, past Glenn's Lumber, Winters' Funeral Home, the Red Door Bar, and McNabb's Hardware. Then, he would cross the small side street to the next block.

Painstakingly, he passed the carwash, Freedom Movie House, Fran's Tag Agency, and Bonnie Lou's Cut and Curl. The block and a half trip took him almost thirty minutes before he reached the door to his main destination – Stephens' Drugstore.

Like most of the stores on Main Street, the drugstore had served the area's patrons almost since the town's founding. Livy's mother, Mary Ann Stephens, graduated pharmacy school and bought the store five years previously in 1971 when Livy was only ten.

Livy took a moment to admire the "Diamonique" rings on her fingers before finally getting up and crossing the black and white tile floor of the store. She took her place behind the soda fountain.

"Can I help you?" she asked the withered man, pretending she had no idea that he was there for the twenty-five-cent coffee he ordered daily.

Old Pete kept his head low, looking only at the counter. "Coffee," came his hoarse and barely audible reply.

As Livy turned to pour his coffee, she watched him in the large picture mirror that hung from the back wall of the fountain. He was the oldest man she had ever seen. His wrinkles were so deep that his walnut brown skin folded in on itself. His small, five-foot four-inch frame looked like it would crumble to dust if he were touched. Still, Livy liked him. He was full of mystery, and his jet-black eyes made him appear to be very wise.

As Livy grabbed a lid for the coffee, she glanced back into the mirror. Doing so caused her image of the mysterious and wise Old Pete to shatter. Pete was pocketing a Slim Jim.

Livy stifled a gasp and instinctively turned away so the time-worn man wouldn't realize that she had seen him. However, as soon as her brain fully comprehended what was unfolding, she turned back to spy.

But Pete wasn't through. He shuffled to a small, round candy carousel on the corner of the fountain bar and quickly shoved a Snickers into the same pocket that held the Slim Jim. It was shocking to the girl how rapidly the feeble fellow moved. It was the quickest thing Livy had ever seen Old Pete do.

Livy had never witnessed a real theft, and her brain went into semi-spasms. Her thoughts raced like ticker tape on Wall Street.

"Oh my God! Old Pete is shoplifting!" her mind relayed, as she tried to make sense of it all.

Livy had no idea how to handle the situation. The last thing she wanted to do was to draw unwanted attention to herself, unless of course, it was from a cute boy.

Livy thought a moment about confronting Old Pete, but that just increased her panic. Doing so might result in catastrophe. After all, Old Pete was already almost dead. Confronting him might give him a heart attack and do him in completely.

The overly dramatic girl took a deep breath to calm herself as she tried to solve her dilemma. *"I should just discretely tell him to pay for them,"* her brain finally reasoned.

"Are you crazy?" her less than sensible self, quickly answered. *"What if he throws the Snickers at you and tries to run? Then, you will have to chase him, and everyone is going to see you!"*

Once Livy ran the entire theoretical episode through her head, she realized any action taken toward Old Pete would probably result in him having a heart attack. Of course, this would serve only in embarrassing her. Her greatest fear was that her latest crush, the high school quarterback, Mitch Stapleton, would hear about the event and think she was a complete dork.

Livy trembled, dreading her own demise and trying to get the nerve to get through her first encounter with a criminal. She realized she needed to do something soon, as Pete was waiting for his coffee. However, she still could not manage to come up with a better scenario than asking him to pay for the items.

She slowly exhaled, and turned with her hands shaking, to set the hot liquid on the counter. As Old Pete produced the quarter to pay for it, she mustered all the courage she could find and hesitantly cleared her throat.

"That will be another forty-five cents for the Slim Jim and Snickers," her voice cracked. Livy felt her heart pounding through her chest as she watched for the archaic man's reaction.

The crumpled old man never looked up to acknowledge her. Instead, he simply picked up his coffee, turned around, and slowly shuffled out the door.

Livy's mouth dropped. She stood silently for a moment trying to decide what to do next. She wondered if she should yell for another employee but then she remembered it would draw attention to herself. She wondered if she should run after him, before remembering that she might cause him to die.

Livy did the only thing she could, which was nothing. She walked to the nearby commercial soda canisters sitting in a small storage area next to the fountain. She slunk down onto the makeshift seat that had been constructed using a cardboard lid from a wholesale box of bubble gum on top of it. She sighed deeply and replayed the entire episode. This caused her to reevaluate her first impressions of Old Pete.

"Wise, my ass," she silently scolded herself. *"Wiseass is more like it."* The newfound assessment caused her to go in search of Ethel, a sassy, sixty-something-year-old clerk who also worked in the store.

Livy found Ethel at the back of the store, gift wrapping an earring tree Mable Bains was purchasing for her granddaughter's birthday.

"You're not going to believe this!" Livy jumped up and down, exaggerating her breathlessness and shock. "Old Pete just stole a Slim Jim and Snickers!" She bugged her eyes to add extra emphasis.

Totally missing the eye popping and greatly disappointing Livy, Ethel ignored the girl and kept wrapping the package. Livy waited only a moment before repeating herself and hearing a response she never expected.

"So?" Ethel calmly answered, still failing to look at the teen.

Livy squinted her eyes and glared hard at Ethel, surmising that the clerk must not have understood, so she re-enacted the entire dramatic scene.

"Ethel," she huffed, "I said Old Pete just stole a Slim Jim and a Snickers bar! He ordered coffee, and when I turned around to get it…" Livy swirled around like a ballerina. "I saw him in the mirror taking the stuff and putting it in his pocket." Livy made a stuffing gesture into one of the pockets of her skin tight hip hugger jeans. "Then I asked him to give me the money for it," she held out an empty hand, "but he just ignored me and walked out!" She stomped her foot on the tile floor.

Ethel, obviously perturbed, set the package down, put her hands on her hips, and turned to the skinny blond girl.

"Livy," she raised a graying eyebrow, "you and your little brother eat more crap from behind that fountain every day than Old Pete eats in a week. Did you ever stop to think that maybe it's the only thing he gets to eat all day?"

Livy felt as if she had just been smacked upside the head. She swallowed hard.

"Ugh…no," the shammed girl stammered, eyeing the floor like a puppy caught peeing on the rug.

The welfare of others wasn't something that had ever penetrated Livy's self-centered sphere of reality. In fact, it hadn't even occurred to the girl that Old Pete might be in need. But since Ethel had so blatantly pointed it out, Livy had no choice but to consider it, and in doing so, her perspective instantly changed. The disgust she once felt for Old Pete redirected itself back upon herself. She felt deeply ashamed.

She hung her humbled head and slowly slunk back to the fountain, the sting of Ethel's admonishment smarting all the way. There she stood, trying to absorb the magnitude of what had unfolded. It didn't take long before she devised a way to make amends where Old Pete was concerned.

From that point forward, when Old Pete ordered coffee, she allowed him to take the extra candy and beef without ever asking him to pay for anything other than the coffee. In fact, even when her mother raised the price of the coffee a couple of years later, Livy continued to charge Old Pete a quarter. It was the least she could do.

Chapter Two

Tubby Anderson

*T*ubby Anderson was a twenty-two-year-old man with an eight-year-old brain. He lived with his mother and father in a trailer house on a little spread of land southeast of town.

Apparently, Tubby oversaw the family's hogs because he repeatedly arrived at the drugstore smelling like an outhouse and wearing crusty denim overalls caked in pig manure.

Livy hated to see him coming because it usually meant she would end up gagging when he, and the green fog that surrounded him, arrived.

Shortly after Livy had returned from receiving Ethel's chastisement, Tubby burst through the door and immediately set his eyes upon the attractive blond as she stood wiping the counters behind the fountain.

"You're purty!" he announced so loudly that even Livy's mother looked up from her glass encased booth at the back of the store.

"Thank you." Livy stopped wiping to see who was paying her the compliment. Seeing it was Tubby, she screwed her face into a torturous twist.

"We should go onna date," the fat, burr headed boy-man declared.

"I have a boyfriend," Livy lied, backing away so she couldn't smell him.

"I kin beat him up." Tubby grinned exposing two holes where teeth used to be, and the nasty, brown, rotted ones that remained. "Who is he?"

"In the first place," Livy hissed, unwilling to completely open her mouth for fear of inhaling Tubby's poisonous odor, "I don't want you to beat him up and, in the second place, it's none of your business who he is."

"You're purty." Tubby wistfully grinned again. "We cud go ta the movie," he persisted.

Livy dropped her rag, put her hands on her hips and glared at Tubby as if he were the devil himself.

"In the first place, I already told you I have a boyfriend," she growled. "And, in the second place, I have already seen the movie," she lied for the second time.

Tubby held up his arm and showed her his bicep muscle. "I kin beat em up!" he repeated.

Livy rolled her eyes, tired of the would-be paramour's antics. "I am not going out with you Tubby. I will never go out with you. There is no world in which I would go out with you. Now, I have stuff to do so you either tell me what you came in here for or go away." She pointed to the front door.

The girl's serious tone and deadly look scared Tubby a little, and he backed away a few feet before answering her.

"Ummm." He shuffled his grimy boots while looking at the floor. "My ma says I need Odor Eaters cause my feet stink." Tubby paused only a moment before trying to balance on one foot while struggling to pull a poop-coated boot off the other. "Wanna smell?"

"No!" Livy screwed her face up again and then put up her hands to stop him. "I'm sure your mom knows what she's talking about. There is no need to prove it." Livy backed away even more, just in case Tubby still thought she needed a demonstration.

"They're over there." Livy pointed to a long wall on the opposite side of the store. "Do you want me to go get them?" she asked, reasoning that it might be the best way to escape the smelly interloper for a few moments.

Tubby shook his head no and turned away from her. "I'll go cus I like ta see all the colors of the bottles on the shelf. I like the Listerine the best."

The astonished look of confusion on Livy's face was immediate and she scratched her head. "You use Listerine?" she queried as if he had told her he could fly.

"Nope." Tubby turned back to her to explain. "I jest like the color. It looks like pee."

Livy shook her head like she was shooing away cobwebs, while she watched Tubby turn again. He walked around the jewelry counter and the middle display aisle separating them. She noticed he was leaving little trails of doop (dirt-poop) behind him.

When Tubby reached the medicine-lined wall, Livy watched his bulbous head bob up and down over the trinkets and porcelain figurines displayed between them. Tubby leisurely strolled past the bottles, stopping every once in a while to take a closer look at them. Finally, he arrived at the

Odor Eater display rack and stood there motionless for several moments.

Livy sighed and returned to wiping the counter when the silence of the store was interrupted by a loud "Bllltttt."

Tubby had farted.

Livy put her hand over her mouth and tried to stifle an embarrassed laugh. Tubby, on the contrary, was rather proud of himself.

"Hey," he gleefully yelled across the store to her, "I farted!"

Livy, her face now three shades of red, could not bring herself to respond.

Tubby turned to address her again, his toothless grin barely visible over the shelves. "Whew!" He waved his hand in front of his face. "That was a good un! I mean bad un!" he boasted.

Livy was nothing short of disgusted, especially when the fart smell mixed with Tubby's despicable body odor finally drifted her way. She decided that she had had enough of his shenanigans and laid into him.

"Tubby, I don't want a play-by-play of your nasty fart!" She shook her finger at him. "You need to get your Odor Eaters and leave this store." She again pointed to the front door before dipping below the fountain and rummaging through the cabinets there.

She had only disappeared for a moment when Tubby saw her pop back up with a can of Lysol and a loud and triumphant "Ah, hah!"

Much to Livy's surprise, Tubby hadn't followed her order to vacate the store. In fact, he hadn't even moved.

"Tubby, I said to get your stuff and leave," she warned him again.

Tubby stood on his tiptoes to get a better look at her. "But I don't know if I should git these here blue uns or these here black uns," he obliviously whined.

Livy clenched her teeth, realizing that in order to get him to leave, she might have to go help him. She only considered the idea for a second before deciding she wasn't willing to risk getting any closer than she already was. Instead, she set aside her fundamental Southern Baptist upbringing and lied for the third time since Tubby had entered the store.

"*Going to hell can't be any worse than Tubby and his smell*," she silently surmised before delivering her latest fib. "Get the black ones. They're for men. The blue are for women." Livy watched Tubby closely to see if he believed her.

"Okie, Dokie." he nodded in agreement, before turning back to the display and pulling off a pair of black ones. He held them up for her to see. "I gots em," he announced as he brought them to the fountain to pay.

When he arrived, Livy thought she would barf as Tubby's odor intensified. She violently turned her head away and reluctantly stuck out her hand. "It's two dollars and fifty-two cents." She released the words in a breathless torrent so she didn't have to inhale his stench. Tubby handed her a dollar and three pennies.

Livy looked at the money while still trying to hold her breath and rolled her eyes again. "Tubby, this isn't enough. You've gotta give me another dollar and forty-nine cents."

Tubby looked back at the money in her hands and bit his lip before looking up at the ceiling as if he were in deep thought. "Ummm, I ain't got it." The simpleton shrugged while pulling out the lining of his revoltingly filthy pockets to show her they were empty. "That there is all Ma give me."

Livy was willing to lose a thousand dollars if it meant getting Tubby out of the store, so she pushed the Odor Eaters across the counter at him.

"Take them and go." She waved her hands, trying to shoo him away.

Tubby didn't budge. Instead, he smiled like a partially toothless chimpanzee.

"If ya want ta go out with me, I'll be back here next Saturday," he half told, half ordered.

Livy raised the can of Lysol and aimed it at him.

"Tubby," she said, pursing her lips, "take your Odor Eaters and go. I. AM. NOT. GOING. OUT. WITH. YOU!"

Tubby stood motionless only a second before Livy pulled the cap off the can and shoved the nozzle mere inches from his face. Realizing she meant business, he pitifully stuck out his bottom lip and pouted in advance of finally turning to go. Livy followed him, spraying billowing clouds of Lysol until he had disappeared.

Chapter Three

Doll Dahl

*L*ivy followed Tubby's trail down the far aisle, spraying Lysol and waving her hands through the air, in a futile attempt to disperse the foul stench that now permeated most of the store.

Her mother eyed her questioningly as she passed the pharmacy.

Livy pinched her nose. "Tubby Anderson stinks like an outhouse!"

Mary Ann thought about her daughter's declaration, nodded her agreement, and then turned back to her work.

Livy continued her spraying up and down the aisles all the while muttering about disgusting pig farmers. When she had fully saturated the air, she went back to the fountain and returned the nearly empty can to its rightful place.

She slid down onto the canisters again and had just propped her feet up on some nearby candy boxes when the morning coffee gang arrived.

She got back up, grabbed the coffee pot, four mugs, and followed them to the last of the four soda tables, which were past the fountain.

"Hi ya, Miss Livy," Festus Marney greeted her. He pulled out an orange metal chair and sat down.

John Davis removed his gray felt cowboy hat and pulled out the royal blue chair across from Festus. Livy filled his cup.

"Did you dance at the game last night, Livy?"

"Yep," Livy answered, a proud smile creeping across her face. She sat the mugs down. "Didn't you go?"

"You know I wouldn't miss a football game girl." He winked his signature wink.

"Then, how come you didn't know I performed with the drill team?" she cocked her head waiting for his reply.

"Cuz, I can't see worth a flip when you youngins are out there prancin' around. Every time I think I've spotted you, you girls whirl and twirl and I've lost you again."

The three other men laughed and nodded their agreement.

John was a stout man. He was six-foot-four. He was one of Livy's very favorite customers because he told her she was pretty and predicted that she would be famous one day. That was music to Livy's ears, because she secretly thought she would be too.

On occasion, John would stay a little longer than the rest of the men and visit with the young lady about things going on around town. He would ask her opinion about this or that. It always made her feel important. But, most days, at precisely 11:30, he would announce to his buddies that his "beautiful bride," who he called Dumplin', would have dinner waiting on him. On those days, he would scoop his hat onto his balding head, leave a quarter on the table, and wink at Livy on his way out.

Livy always wondered why John and the older folks, including her grandparents, used the word dinner for lunch and supper for dinner. It was something she never learned.

Livy turned to Fred Gladden, who had chosen the yellow chair, and filled his cup. Then, she filled Boomer Daws' while he was claiming the green one

Festus Marney looked up at her when she began to fill his. "Looks like it's extra hot." He smiled.

"The only good coffee is hot coffee," John added.

The four regulars usually stayed a couple of hours every day to drink coffee and solve the world's dilemmas. Livy liked to eavesdrop on their conversations, and she learned a lot about the goings-on in town just from listening in every Saturday. Normally the group talked farming, town politics, or football. But this day, they started right in discussing the Great Senior Citizen Crime Spree.

For the previous three months, someone had been robbing the town's elderly residents. The weekly newspaper said two women, one, middle aged, and the other in her mid-twenties, had been stealing money and valuables. The women told the unsuspecting Good Samaritans that they were having car trouble and asked to use the phone. Once they gained entrance, they would tie up their victims and rob them. Even her Grandmother Stephens had almost been a victim, but she had the foresight not to let them into her house.

Luckily, the perpetrators had not harmed anyone while robbing them, but the town's residents were concerned that it was only a matter of time before someone would get hurt.

What was most bothersome to the townsfolk, however, was the fact that Lester, the town's only police officer, had not been able to solve the crime spree. The invasions were all anyone had been talking about, including who they thought could be the guilty party.

Livy told the men to holler if they needed a refill, and she went back behind the fountain to sit down again. She had only been seated a moment before the glass door swung open to reveal the town's resident movie star, Doll Dahl.

The eccentric, wannabe starlet came sweeping in and threw her arm into the air dramatically announcing her arrival. She stopped and scanned the store and then began waving to non-existent admirers as if she were Miss America. After only a short moment, she started shooing the same make-believe admirers away from her.

"Enough!" the gangly woman announced. "I just want some peace!" She sighed exasperatingly before turning to look at her seventy-something-year-old mother who had followed her into the store. Doll helped her mother inside the door before turning again, glaring at emptiness in front of her and bringing a cigarette stylus (minus the cigarette) to her lips. She took a long, imaginary drag and loudly exhaled it. She brushed back a white feather boa that hung around her neck and down her shoulder over a light blue, floor-length, chiffon dress which was sparsely adorned with iridescent sequins. Her outfit was completed with a pair of well-worn, aquamarine satin pumps, topped with tufts of dirty marabou.

Doll Dahl's head was held back high exposing bright blue eye shadow layered to the top of her eyebrows, dark red rouge, streaked up her cheeks, and crimson colored lipstick. The lipstick had been applied not only on her lips and teeth but halfway up to her nose on her skin. The outcome was clown-like, making it appear as if she had been terribly drunk when applying it.

The first time Livy had seen Doll Dahl, she was around twelve. Livy was nothing short of enthralled. Doll had sauntered into the store, exactly as she had done this day. She surveyed the entire place before going to the fountain and telling her mother to order her a Coca-Cola. Her mother obliged while Doll nonchalantly fingered the candy bar carousel.

Doll Dahl had a breathy, throaty, husky voice. Livy couldn't take her eyes off the strange and infatuating woman. When Livy neglected to release her gaze from the woman, Doll's mother angrily glared at her.

Alberta, a persnickety and holier-than-thou type of woman was Livy's least favorite of the store's clerks. When Alberta noticed the mother's annoyance, she shoved Livy out of the way and took the order herself.

Livy, oblivious to her own rudeness, had remained mesmerized until the moment the flamboyant woman and her mother left.

"Who was that?" she had excitedly asked Alberta before beginning a tirade of rapid fire questions. "Did you see her makeup? Did you see what she was wearing? Oh, my God, she was scary - in a cool sort of way. Who was she? Where…"

"If you'll shut your pie hole for two whole seconds," Alberta interrupted, "I'll tell you."

Livy closed her mouth, and Alberta relayed the woman's story. She told Olivia that Doll's real name was Trudy Dahl and she had once been one of the most beautiful girls in the area. She said that she had loved acting in the school plays and wanted to go to New York or Hollywood and become a famous actress. However, before graduating, Trudy fell in love with a boy from Ashton, a small town about ten miles away. The two became inseparable for a couple of years until one day, out of the blue, the boy broke up with her. Alberta said that Trudy went crazy and began believing she was already a famous actress. At that point, she demanded that everyone call her by her stage name – Doll.

Alberta went on to preach to Livy that she was "horribly and emphatically appalled" that the town's residents went along with the ruse.

Livy, on the other hand, thought it was fantastic. She relished the exoticness of the story and loved it when Doll "made an appearance" so that she, too, could be part of the charade. It was one of the few things that Livy felt combated the ever-present boredom of the one-horse town.

This Saturday, after Doll Dahl had tired of her admirers, she led her mother to the fountain, regally swaying her head side to side.

"Ma Ma," she crooned in her sultry voice, "please order me a Coca-Cola. Oh, and have them add some cherry." She daintily pointed her stylus to the syrups behind the fountain as if she was waving a magic wand.

"Yes, dear," her silver haired mother obliged.

Livy was already scooping the ice before Doll's mother could parrot the request. "Right away Miss Dahl," Livy directed her reply to the starlet. "How are you today?"

"Ma Ma," Doll looked down at her petite mother, "Tell her I am well."

Again, Livy did not wait for Doll's mother. "That is just lovely. You look stunning today and your dress is spectacular," Livy gushed.

Doll tilted her nose up in the air and ignored her young admirer. Then, she ordered her elderly mother to pay for the drink.

"Enjoy," Livy smiled to the peculiar thespian.

Doll's mother turned and escorted her to the first of the soda tables, leaving two between her and the coffee gang.

"I'm going to fill my prescriptions dear. Will you wait on me here?" she asked the starlet as she patted her daughter's fluffy shoulder.

Doll Dahl swished her boa behind her neck, dramatically brushed nonexistent crumbs from a blue metal soda chair, and sat down to sip her soda.

The coffee gang all turned to notice her and the pretending ensued.

"Beautiful day, Miss Dahl," Boomer said, tipping his ball cap to the woman.

"Surprised you are in town today and not in Hollywood," Fred chimed in.

"My, aren't you pretty today," Festus added.

"Prettier than all those other movie stars," John declared.

Doll Dahl coolly ignored them all, although, she did manage to hiss "Peasants," under her breath. Livy wondered if Doll might also believe that she was royalty.

Doll Dahl fidgeted for a while, pretending not to pay any attention to the men; although she would discreetly glance at them from time to time. In turn, they would politely nod.

However, when the men resumed their discussion, Doll realized they were not going to ask for her autograph. She humphed and stood up, leaving her cherry Coke on the table. She flung her boa back again and made her way to a greeting card display behind her. There, she fingered several cards with fake interest while periodically taking a "puff" from the stylus. Every few moments, she would peer over her shoulder again to see if the men were paying her any attention. They weren't. She humphed again.

Livy watched Doll from the corner of her eye, trying not to be too conspicuous. Doll had once again returned her gaze to the cards and was intently reading one which had a big, red foil heart above a man and woman who were obviously getting married. It was only a moment before Livy saw Doll pull a lace handkerchief from her bosom and dab her eyes. Livy wondered what it was that had upset the woman when Doll whipped around to face the back of the store.

"Go! I want to go!" she yelled, startling not only Livy but also the four seated men who turned to watch the outburst. Doll stomped her feet one at a time, the dusty blue marabou flopping up and down.

"I said," her foot hit the floor with a thwack. "I want," her other foot followed, "To GO!"

Doll's mother came running from the back and grabbed her. She patted her shoulder, attempting to calm her.

"Oh, my," the matriarch said, turning her daughter away from the cards and looking back at John and his friends as if apologizing. "Of course, my dear. We'll go right now." She took Doll's face into her hands and looked her in the eyes.

"We'll go right now," Doll's mother nodded her head, trying to get Doll to focus on her. "Right now," she said again. She took Doll by the shoulders and turned her toward the front door.

The older woman led the sequin-clad daughter past the fountain.

When she reached the door, she called back to Livy, "Tell your mother I will be back for the prescriptions later."

"Okay," Livy murmured, wondering what the heck just happened.

Chapter Four

The Tinsleys

*L*ivy noticed that some of Tubby's dirt trail was still in front of the fountain. She grabbed a broom and swept it up. Then, she sat back down on a soda canister and waited for her next customer. After several minutes with nothing to do, she became bored and decided to redecorate one of the store's front two display windows.

Livy crawled into the window closest to the fountain and began removing the smoking pipes, cigar tins, and other various tobacco products. Livy could still see some shards of glass that had not been cleaned up from a break-in by a Tinsley several months earlier.

Livy's hometown, Konawa (pronounced Con-uh-wah), Oklahoma was home to about thirty mentally disabled people who resided at Tinsley's Nursing Home. The townsfolk didn't usually refer to the inhabitants by name, but instead called them all Tinsleys.

Once a week, Livy had to deliver prescriptions to the nursing home. She would have preferred to streak down Main Street naked. As far as she was concerned, there was nothing – no thing – worse than delivering to Tinsley's, because some of the tenants scared the living bejeebers out of her.

As soon as Livy walked through the nursing home door, the residents swarmed her. Some petted her; some drooled on her; and others grabbed her. They followed her all the way to the nurse's station, each battling the other to get close to her. When she wanted to leave, she had to sprint toward the door, trying in vain to escape them. They were often very organized however, making her escape next to impossible. The offending group would build an impenetrable wall with their bodies. Livy would look for a hole. She'd dodge one participant, just to have another block her path. Eventually, one of the aides would see the assembly and rescue her.

"Go to your rooms!" the employee would yell, pointing them down the hall. "You should all be ashamed of yourselves," she would scold. It didn't faze the Tinsleys though. They would just smile at their chiding overseer before skipping off.

THE DRUGSTORE

Several of the less afflicted Tinsleys were allowed out of the home under their own supervision. They came to town and wandered through the stores, sometimes buying a soda or something from the Five and Dime. They were usually welcomed as, more or less, a normal thread in the town's fabric.

The most well-known of all the Tinsleys was Trucker. Trucker was a dwarfish, roly-poly, bald fellow who stood about five feet two inches. The hair Trucker did have was gray and stuck out like the fluff under a chicken's butt. He had a pug nose, big pock marks on his cheeks, and a perpetual shadow of gray stubble on his chin.

Trucker couldn't speak normally. Instead, he grunted-growled through clenched little baby like teeth; making what were akin to 'Errrrr' noises. Understanding any part of what Trucker was trying to say was about as likely as kindergartener understanding quantum physics.

Trucker got his name because anytime he saw a parked pickup truck, he climbed into the bed and waited for the owner to give him a ride. There were only a few people in town who would acquiesce to his demands. The majority ordered him to get out. Most of the time, Trucker would go peacefully

"Erring" his disdain. But other times, if he was in a foul mood, he would spit at the person who had refused him.

That really pissed off the old-timers. They would scream and cuss at Trucker, calling him a bastard. Unfortunately, their tirades only led to the ornery scamp spitting at them again, which, in turn, led to the old timers threatening to whip him. Only when Trucker realized he might be in danger, would he reluctantly jump from the bed. Of course, that wouldn't happen before he had unabashedly "Errred" at his nemesis.

Although Trucker was never one of the residents of Tinsley's Nursing Home that liked to fawn over Livy, he once played a role in making a delivery hellish for her younger brother, Sam.

Often, because the Stephens' had to pass Tinsley's to get to their house, they made deliveries to the establishment on their way home. One day, Mary Ann had driven her husband's pickup truck, and not realizing the ramifications that could befall them, she drove up to the entrance and parked. She told Livy, who had been riding in the bed with Sam to take the prescriptions inside.

Trucker, who was mingling by the front door, took one look at the bed occupied by the two and went ballistic, thinking they were impeding on his truck bed territory. Livy, fully comprehending what was about to take place, immediately jumped out of the truck. Sam, who was apparently oblivious to Trucker's less than reasonable demeanor, kept his seat.

Trucker approached Sam, eyes bulging from his head.

"Errr…errr…er…errrr!" he yelled while leaning over the side of the truck and grabbing Sam's arm, trying to force him out. Sam, looked at Livy wondering why the Tinsley was grabbing him, but he continued to stay where he was.

That infuriated Trucker, and seeing that he wasn't able to force Sam out, Trucker instead jumped in.

As soon as he steadied himself, he glared at Sam, made little fists and began dancing around.

"Errr…errr…err…er!" Trucker spat, while prancing, and apparently challenging Sam to a fist fight.

Finally understanding his predicament, Sam yelled to his mother to get Trucker out of the bed. Mary Ann, also being highly aware of Trucker's questionable disposition, got out of the cab, and tried to intimidate the miniature boxer.

"Trucker, you come down from there right now!" she hollered, as if that was going to work. Trucker ignored her. Instead, he bent over and grabbed Sam by the collar. Seeing that her demands had no effect and fearing that her son might become Trucker's latest victim, or worse, Trucker might become Sam's first, Mary Ann screamed at Livy to get a nurse. Livy, knowing what awaited her in the crowded hallways, refused.

"I told you to GO GET THE NURSE!" Mary Ann shoved Livy toward the front door of Tinsley's. "Or else!" she added so that Livy would realize that it was either face the Tinsleys or become grounded.

Livy figured she could avoid both, and instead yelled down the hall, "Hey, we need help out here!"

A small crowd of Tinsleys had been gathering. They were whooping, hollering, and jumping up and down. This gave Trucker, even more incentive to fight.

Seeing no help in sight, Mary Ann got into the back of the truck and tried to pull Trucker out. It was at that point that Sam decided he had enough.

Although Sam was a year younger than Livy, he was six feet two inches tall and played linebacker on the junior varsity football team. Livy saw Sam's eyes fill with rage before he let out a guttural, animalistic roar and got to his feet.

Previously, Trucker had not stopped to size up his great enemy. But once Sam had emerged fully upright, Trucker was able to see the very large, very wide, and very angry boy whom he had been assaulting.

Trucker's eyes got as big as saucers, and he stopped his pummeling mid-blow. He began to back away. "Errr...errr...er" he said apologetically while reaching for the tailgate in order to steady himself enough to climb out.

Sam, still in the heat of the moment, lunged. He fully intended to thrash the pint-sized nuisance, but Mary Ann grabbed him just in time.

"Get ahold of yourself," she admonished. "These are my customers."

Sam, still seething, reluctantly sat back down but never took his glaring eyes off Trucker. Trucker too, kept his eyes on Sam. However, it was to make sure he wasn't going to get jumped from behind.

Trucker slunk over to the facility's front porch and tried disappearing into the enthralled crowd. Only then did the charge nurse appear, slamming through the door, and headlong into the cluster of Tinsleys.

"Just what the heck is goin' on out here?!" she demanded of the group. The gathered Tinsleys, along with Livy and Mary Ann, pointed to Trucker.

After Mary Ann explained what had taken place, the nurse chastised the trouble-maker.

Trucker, however, sensing that the danger had passed, strutted past her, snickering. "Errr...er...err," he sneered, which seemed to mean "Kiss my ass."

Livy looked at the small piece of glass that had remained in the window and tossed it aside, remembering the incident which produced it. Several months earlier, on a Sunday when the town's stores were closed, a Tinsley named Peanut decided to take a stroll up Main Street. As he passed Stephens' Drugstore, he spied a cherry wood tobacco pipe in the window. Peanut was so enamored with the pipe that he couldn't wait until Monday to buy it. Instead, he picked up a brick, that was normally used to prop the door open on nice afternoons, and heaved it through the window. The Tinsley climbed through the broken mess and took the pipe, leaving a small wad of money in the window case to pay for it.

But the damage he had done was far beyond what it would take to replace the window. It was shortly after the delivery episode, and the breaking of the window, that a third incident occurred. Another Tinsley walked into the football coach's house and put himself to bed. When the multiple complaints surfaced, Mr. Tinsley was forced to forbid his residents from going into town by themselves anymore and the Tinsleys' wandering days came to an end.

After that, once a week, a small bus brought the residents, accompanied by their aides into the town to shop. As strange as it seemed, it was upsetting to Livy. Without the daily presence of the Tinsleys, and the shenanigans they brought with them, there had been a hole left in the far too quickly changing landscape of the town.

Chapter Five

Real Crime

Main Street was the only street in town that anyone referred to by name. Anytime directions were given, it was by use of landmarks. If someone unfamiliar with Konawa asked how to find someone or something, they were told, "Just go to the end of the street, take a left at the gas station, and you'll find it across from the little church on the corner."

Although the town had been much larger during the turn of the century and through the late 1950's, a large tornado changed that. In February of 1961, two-thirds of the town's businesses were destroyed. Most people didn't rebuild or reopen their shops. If they did, they moved fifteen miles southeast to Maiden, where there was a larger population, and therefore, more patrons.

Also, when the Katy Railroad took the town off its route, that was pretty much the end of growth. After the storm, with the exception of the two grocery stores, three gas station and convenience stores, almost every merchant that remained, had no competition – including the drugstore.

Konawa had been named by the Seminole Indian Tribe. It was settled when, prior to becoming a state in 1907, Oklahoma was still Indian Territory. The word Konawa means "String of Beads," which was a form of currency for the tribe.

The little community is located about 70 miles southeast of Oklahoma City, the state's capital. In 1976, Konawa had a population of one thousand, nine hundred, and ninety-one residents, and even that included folks that lived five miles outside of town.

The main street ran north and south. It was formally named Broadway but always called "Main," because almost all of the stores were located there. There was also the real Main Street, which ran east and west where Broadway ended. Harvey's affronted it, looking over a circular and grassy median, with a tall flagpole in the middle.

The median and the flagpole were often a source of entertainment for the kids in town who, because of their boredom, used it to torment Lester. Livy's older sister, Carrie, was a repeat offender.

Lester was a natural target. He was big – really big, to the tune of about three hundred and fifty pounds. He was also very short.

The majority of Lester's time was spent sitting in the gravel parking lot of Harvey's in his beatup patrol car. If Lester was not sleeping, he was watching people drive by while spitting tobacco out his window. At around five every evening, he would go home and leave the town defenseless. That is when Livy's sister and her cohorts turned into mischief makers.

Carrie and her friends enjoyed decorating the circular island for special occasions, and sometimes, for no occasion at all. Every Christmas, the city would string lights from the top of the flag pole, angling them to the ground to form a tree.

Carrie and her allies assembled at her house. They would partake of Boone's Farm Strawberry Hill wine before sneaking into town to steal several lights from the tree. The strands were the kind that would not stay lit if any were missing or broken, so the following day, Lester would have to hunt through each strand to find the missing ones and replace them. It was comical to witness the fat little man, balancing on a step ladder, in the middle of the median, while cars drove past and honked at him.

Because of the hardship, Lester would lay in wait the nights following his ordeal. But, of course, the teenage offenders would never show. Eventually, he would let down his guard and go home, only to have the culprits repeat their prank.

One of the group's best pranks caused the town's only traffic jam. The sly group found an old toilet in an abandoned house and a broken mannequin torso behind the Western Wear store. They put the toilet at the base of the flagpole and placed the mannequin in it with its arms up as if it was flailing about.

The next morning, Lester, with the police car's lights flashing, pulled up to the circle as a small crowd gathered in front of the stores to watch him try to dismantle it. The base of the mannequin's torso was stuck in the bowl, leaving Lester tugging and pulling to release it. After half an hour with no success, he told Mr. Glenn from the lumber store to call the police station and have the city janitor bring him a hammer. Cars pulled around the circle and parked to watch Lester pound on the bowl chipping little pieces away. Drivers clapped and whistled when Lester finally pulled the plastic body free and loaded it and the commode into the trunk of his cruiser.

He assailed the assembled crowd. "Get on yer way!" Then, he waddled back to his car, mumbling and cussing under his breath.

It was those types of juvenile pranks that made up the majority of "crime" in town until the Senior Citizen Crime Spree started. Word on the street was that Lester, after receiving a lot of pressure from some prominent citizens and a few clergy whose parishioners had been victimized, finally called in the Oklahoma State Bureau of Investigation to help him track down the culprits.

Several people, including the drugstore's coffee gang, had talked about where, if caught, the guilty women would be housed. Konawa's jail couldn't even qualify as minimum security. There were only two cells positioned at the back of City Hall. They sat adjacent to the back door and were separated by a four-foot-wide hallway.

In summer, because there was no air-conditioning, a screen door was used to let the air circulate. The door had a little hook and eye latch and nothing more. Anyone wanting to make a jail break could easily have done so. However, considering most of those housed were patrons of the Red Door Bar, and seemed perfectly content serving their time by sleeping off their benders, it had never been tested.

Boomer and the gang seemed pretty excited that the culprits would probably end up at a big-time jail, like the four cell county jail, twenty miles away.

One thing was for sure, the crime spree was the biggest thing to have happened in the town since the tornado of 1961, and although it gave folks something to talk about, it had worn out its welcome. There wasn't anyone around that wasn't ready for it to be solved – and soon.

Chapter Six

Bengal Billy

here was a lot to be seen from Livy's perch in the drugstore window. Across the street, a tall, lanky man with long black Brylcreemed hair was walking beside his sweetheart who was riding a bike. She was a plump, little, round thing with equally long, black hair. The town's people had named them Romeo and Juliet. On this day, they were out doing their grocery shopping at Pendleton's IGA.

As Juliet stopped the ancient bicycle, Romeo held her steady and helped her lift her dress so she wouldn't catch it on the seat. He bent over her squatty frame and kissed her forehead. He propped the bike up against the big ice freezer in front of the store and rushed to open the door for his beloved.

Sometimes, the two would go into the drugstore and have an ice cream soda. He smelled of sweat and Old Spice. She smelled of roses. They would sit at a table, sip their soda, and giggle like school children. He would brush the hair from her face while longingly looking into her eyes. She would blush.

After they finished their sodas, he would pull her chair out for her, clasp her arm, and escort her back to the bicycle. She would get on and ride, and he would walk beside her to wherever they had come from originally.

When the two had disappeared into Pendleton's, Livy noticed Bengal Billy coming out of the Red Door Bar with his three sidekicks. They were all three wagging their tails and trying to pull him in different directions. Each one was mangier than the next.

Bengal Billy had a thing for dogs. Any stray dog he could find became his. And for some very strange reason, he liked to dress them up. He would steal women's clothing from various clotheslines around town and proceed to adorn each furry creature in a variety of garments. One would wear a tank top, the other a pair of shorts, and on several occasions, they might be seen in a bra and panties.

It wasn't unusual for ladies to see him and the dogs in town with their own clothing that had gone missing days before. The theft victim would pull up to the police station and tell Lester that they had just seen their clothing going by on the mutts. None of the women had the guts to confront Billy face-to-face. They were sure he was crazy and didn't want to take any chances.

Most of the time, Lester let it slide because he couldn't prove that Billy had actually stolen the clothing.

"This ole thing?" Billy would say. "I found this here next to the train tracks." And Lester couldn't rightfully say he hadn't, so the thieving and the dressing of his dogs continued.

Billy gave all the dogs female names, even if they weren't female. He brought them to town regularly, especially when he was drunk. On this day, he had Darlene, Earlene, and Ernestine in tow.

Billy had once been a golden gloves boxer in the lightweight division. He had made a real name for himself. He got the name Bengal Billy because he was a real tiger in the ring.

No one was sure what had changed his path so drastically. Most assumed it was a stint in the Army where he had been seriously injured while serving in Vietnam. He had been honorably discharged after the injury, which left him with a significant limp.

When Billy came home after the war, he didn't know what to do with himself. He possessed both the injury and what could only be described as a questionable emotional state.

It was obvious he had a good heart because he took excellent care of his dogs. Throughout the years, he had collected them, feeling sorry for any stray that came his way. Sometimes, he and his furry companions, could be found at the Eater Upper Drive-In. Billy would buy each of them, and himself, a cheeseburger. The pack would eat in the parking lot while Billy leaned against the side of the building to help support himself.

Other times, he might be seen at the town's small park, rolling and jumping in the leaves with his companions. However, when Billy had been drinking, it was easy to forget he had such a soft heart because his mouth was as foul as any sailor's.

Livy watched Billy stumble-limping down the street with the dogs. The closer he got to Livy's window, the louder she could hear his ranting.

"Geeet the hell over here," he yelled at the dog in pink underwear, which was determined to go its own way.

"You're just a big ole dumb ass," he said pointing to the offending party. "I don't know why I even take..." he trailed off while staggering into the brick façade of Fran's.

"I don't know why..." he tried again, "I even try and take you summa bitches to town. You's jest always," he staggered

toward the street. "Yous jest always messi, messin' up things…
summa bitches," he repeated.

While he was making his way closer to Livy's window,
she began wondering if she ought to get out of it so she didn't
scare him to death when he came by.

She need not have worried. Billy was totally oblivious to
her while he struggled to stay upright and keep the dogs from
tangling their homemade rope leashes around his legs.

"Damn dogs," he said, pointing at all three of them now.
"Oh but you sure, you surearrr purty!" He threw his head back
and cackled.

This action threw him so far off balance that he fell into
the iron gate that sealed off a stairwell which led to the top
floor of the drugstore. Billy hit the gate with his back and then
slid down until his butt hit the sidewalk.

"Oh great," Livy said to herself while climbing out of the
window. "He's going to pass out right here in front of the
store."

Livy called to Ethel who was making sweet pickles behind
the fountain.

"Bengal Billy just fell into the gate. What should we do?"
she asked.

The dogs were all circling him now, whining, nosing him, and licking his face.

"Oh hell," said Ethel, "just call over to the police station. Tell Lester to come get em. Maybe, he can let him sleep it off."

Livy went to the phone while Ethel peered out the window.

"Wait a minute, he's getting up," Ethel called.

Livy went back to the window and watched the very inebriated man try and unwrap himself from the leashes. The dogs continued jumping back and forth over him and tying him every which way but loose.

"Summma bitches," he mumbled while trying to get up.

Billy managed to untangle one knee and steady himself on it, but to no avail. He fell back onto his butt, sitting on one of the leashes. Earlene, the dog attached to it, tried to free herself but only managed in scooting Billy a little down the sidewalk making him even madder.

"You GD summa bitches," he yelled. "Dumb ass dogs," he continued while falling onto his side.

"Earlene stop your movin! Can't you see I'mma... I'mma tryin' to get my ass up?" he asked one who was dressed in shorts.

"Go call Lester," Ethel said. "There is no way in hell he is going to get up."

She was right. Billy rolled back over after talking to Earlene. He laid there with one eye half open, and the other trying to focus on anything.

"Hey," he finally spoke. "I need a beer. Can one you summa bitches go and get me a damn beer?"

The dogs ignored his request and continued to nose and lick him.

In the meantime, Lester, in his wrinkled police uniform and semi-high-water pants, waddled across the street yelling at Billy to get off the sidewalk.

Billy, of course, didn't and continued to lay there looking around with one eye.

"Come on, Billy," Lester said untangling him while helping him to his feet. "It's time to visit Lula," which is what Lester called the jail.

"Okay," said Billy, staggering to his feet. "Can you get me a damn beer before we go?" he queried.

"Maybe later, Champ," Lester answered, dragging him back across the street.

"You all get," Lester told the dogs. They ignored him and followed their master to the jail.

THE DRUGSTORE

They obviously knew the routine from having done it so many times because they looped around to the back of City Hall. They laid down next to the screen door and curled up together to wait for Billy's release.

Chapter Seven

Young Love

Crawling back into the window, Livy began hanging cardboard cutout fall leaves from the ceiling by fishing line. This trick made the leaves appear as if they were floating. Fall was upon the town, and the high school football season was in full swing.

The town lived for football. Every Friday night, the entire population, except for the shut-ins and Tinsleys, attended the game. If the game was out of town, stores would close early so people had plenty of time to travel and get to the rival school before kickoff. Those days Main Street took on the appearance of a ghost town, and the once bustling community, stood dark and silent.

A bright silver flash caught Livy's eye as she rose to tie another leaf. It was Mitch, the man of her dreams – at least the current one – and his best friend, Pogo. The two went screeching by the store in Mitch's 1975 Silver Camaro with Pogo's lily-white and naked rear end hanging out the passenger side window. As Pogo mooned the town, he and Mitch were whooping and hollering something about kicking ass. Livy assumed they were yelling about the game the previous night when Konawa's football team beat Stelter forty-two to fourteen.

Stelter wasn't the school's main rival, but they were in the top three. Playing them was like playing ping-pong. One year, Konawa would win, the next year Stelter would take it. It went back and forth like that for years. This year was the home team's.

Pogo was a big guy, and he played tackle. He got his name because he was constantly jumping around when he was on the field and looked like a pogo stick. It didn't matter if he was on the sidelines during offensive play, or if he was lining up on defense to take someone out, he just couldn't stay still. The coaches never minded his jumping around though. On several occasions, he caused the other team penalties.

Because of his quick, startling movements, the opposing team would think the ball was in play. He had managed more than a few times to get the other team a false start penalty on third down making it nearly impossible to get the first down.

As it turned out, Pogo became one of the team's best secret weapons.

Although Pogo was a big guy, he didn't have the brains to match. He was pretty slow upstairs and could be talked into almost anything. Showing his shiny hiney off on Main Street was calm compared to some of the other stunts he performed.

The football guys knew with just a little coaxing they could get him to do their dirty work. But, it was clear that Pogo never really thought their ideas through. If he had, he surely wouldn't have gone along with some of the more vengeful acts. He wasn't mean spirited, just naive.

One night, Mitch and the first string wide receiver, Jake, known as Jakey, talked Pogo into soaping a big fountain at the Worster place. Old Man Worster was the richest man in the county. He had a huge spread west of town with a gigantic mansion in the middle of it. In the center of the circle driveway was an enormous decorative garden fountain. It had three tiers and reached halfway to the second story of the house. Concrete lions flanked each of the four sides, and a giant urn sat atop, spewing several columns of water that cascaded to the bowls below.

Over half the working people in town were employed by Old Man Worster, including Jakey's dad who had recently been "laid off." Being laid off was Old Man Worster's way of firing people. Worster never called it firing, because there was barely enough of a workforce in town to maintain his operations. So, as soon as he forgot why he fired someone, or the trouble had blown over and he needed help, the offending party was brought back into the fold.

This time, Jakey's daddy had been the target, and Jakey was out for revenge. Jakey and Mitch talked Pogo into sneaking up the driveway in the middle of the night and filling the fountain full of Amway dishwashing detergent. Pogo used the whole bottle, and the next morning the entire lawn, driveway, and cars were covered with soapsuds.

When the sprinklers came on things got even worse. Old Man Worster had to wade through soap suds thigh high just to get to his Cadillac. He pulled out on the road, leaving a bubbly trail all the way to the car wash where he spent over an hour trying to rinse the soap from the car. Amazingly, it managed to keep bubbling, and Worster had to give up and go to work. His shiny black Cadillac never looked as shiny after that. Instead, it had taken on a dull, lusterless finish from the soap film, which had baked on in the hot Oklahoma sun.

Old Man Worster hadn't been the juvenile delinquents' only victim. After Mitch and two other football players got paddled (licks as they were called), for skipping school, they had Pogo help them wage revenge on Mr. Walter, the high school principal. The boys were ruthless to the poor man, toying with him for over a month.

The first payback came when they put his Pinto in neutral and let it roll down the sloping parking lot to the football field. They pushed the car through the large entrance gate and stored it behind the concession stand where it was completely hidden from sight. That afternoon, when Mr. Walter left the school, his car was nowhere to be found. He called Lester and reported it stolen. Mr. Walter had to walk home and back to school for a couple of days until the junior class sponsors discovered it when they had to get the concession stand ready for Friday's game.

The next payback for the unsuspecting principal came when the spiteful pranksters hid a pair of ladies' black panties under the driver's seat of his car. As much as he tried to deny not knowing where they came from, or why they were under his car seat, Mr. Walter's wife didn't buy it. It was rumored he spent the next three weeks on the couch. And, to make matters worse, Pogo in his best high-pitched girl's voice, would call his house late at night and ask Mrs. Walter if Mr. Walter could come out and play.

The football boys and Pogo finally left poor Mr. Walter alone after informing the town by way of the school marquee, that "MR WALTER SUCKS GREEN DONKEY DICKS."

Mitch and Pogo, with his pants now pulled up, drove up to the First Baptist Church, where the stores ended and made a U-turn. Mitch was swigging an I.B.C. Root Beer, which looked like a real beer bottle, making the teen think he looked cool.

Pogo was downing a Big Red and slumping back into the black vinyl passenger seat.

"Mitch is so gorgeous," Livy mentally noted while watching the two pass by for the second time. *"Is he ever going to ask me out?"*

Her romantic daydreaming was abruptly interrupted by her best friend, Stevy. "Hey Livy, what are you doing?"

Livy jumped, nearly falling face first into the window. "Dang it to Hades, Stevy, you just scared the living crap out of me."

"Sorry, I scared you," Stevy apologized, shrugging her shoulders.

"That's okay," Livy, obliged while crawling down. "Come on, I'll make you a Suicide."

Suicides were Livy's specialty. They consisted of every single flavor kept behind the fountain all mixed together to form a syrupy, tangy, fizzy, test tube, laboratory-looking cola.

"Bebe's gonna be here in a minute," Stevy said while Livy shot the syrups into a glass.

Bebe was the class clown and was always saying or doing something funny. The group planned to meet up and scheme about how Bebe, who had her eye on Jakey, and Livy could become members of the "I have a boyfriend" club. About the time Livy finished making the Suicide, Bebe walked in.

"Hey, what's up beside the panties in my crack," Bebe snorted.

"You're so sick," Livy said, acting like it wasn't funny at all. "I don't know why we hang out with you. You're such a dork."

"It's because I'm so utterly superior and breathtaking and marvelous," Bebe said. She fluttered her eyelashes and quivered her lip, then tossed in a sexy Marilyn Monroe-like shoulder roll.

"Yeah, yeah," Stevy interrupted. "You are just the Queen of Sheba, aren't you?"

"Now girls, play nice," Livy motioned for them to sit at the table that Doll Dahl had abandoned. "Guess what? I just saw Mitch drive down Main. He's with Pogo. Pogo mooned the whole town."

"That is just gross," Stevy said, curling her upper lip.

"Ewww, yeah," Bebe agreed.

"I know. He's such a dork sometimes." Livy nodded. "Okay, focus. How are we going to get Mitch and Jakey to ask us out?" She turned to Bebe.

"You could have your brother set you up with Mitch," Stevy offered.

Livy rolled her eyes. "I seriously doubt that will work. I can hear him now, 'Ha, ha, ha! Like Mitch Stapleton would have anything to do with a little freshman. Stay away from my friends Livy, or I'll beat the crap out of you,'" she impersonated.

The three girls sat a few more moments, trying to come up with a plan. Finally, Livy sat up and slammed her hand on the table.

"I bet they are going to be dragging Main in Maiden tonight," she jumped a little with excitement. "Are you and Brandon going?" she asked Stevy, realizing she might be the answer to their prayers.

"I haven't talked to him yet. But if we go, we could drop you guys off at Hardee's, and you could just hang out there and see if they come in."

"Woohoo, Bebe! Looks like we have a plan!" Livy jumped up and down in her chair.

"I'll have to ask my mom," Bebe, sulked, killing the enthusiasm. "She's really been horrible lately. I think she's going through mean-o-pause. I swear I have been hiding in my room for days because she is so cranky." Bebe scowled. "I got home five minutes late last night, and she told me if I did it again, she would ground me so long that I would be farting dust before it was over."

"Holy cow," Livy said, raising an eyebrow.

Bebe proceeded to elaborate on just how badly her mother's hormones were wreaking havoc.

"You should see what she's been doing to my poor dad. He asked her to pass the potatoes, and she told him to get his lily-livered ass up and get them himself." She shook her head. "Then she got up and walked off mumbling something about having to do everything but take a dump for him." "And thennnnn,"Bebe strung out the words for emphasis, "she said she might as well do that so she wouldn't have to clean skid marks out of his underwear!"

Stevy twisted her face. "Ewwww, that is just gross!"

"I'm telling you," Bebe assured, "If she doesn't do something soon about her mood swings, somebody is going to die. It could be me. It could be my sister. It could be my dad. But mark my words, somebody is going to die."

"Well, ask her anyway." Livy smiled, trying to lighten Bebe's mood. "Tell her you are going to spend the night with me. She will probably be glad to get rid of you."

"Okay, I'll see. But don't hold your breath. There's a new sheriff in town, and she makes Lester look like a pink tutu-wearin', flower-pickin', sissy boy."

Chapter Eight

Ethel and Alberta

The girls were still sitting at the table gossiping about really important issues like why Rhonda Granger kept wearing bell-bottom jeans when they were so yesterday and gloating about how the high school football players thought the ninth-grade cheerleading squad – of which they were all members – was better than the varsity team.

Alberta made her fourth trip by the tables to glare at Livy and not-so-subtlety let her know she did not like that she was not manning the fountain. Livy ignored her, knowing that Ethel was taking care of it.

Alberta and Ethel were about as different as ice cream and sardines. The only thing even remotely similar about the two was that they were both in their sixties. Even that was a stretch considering Ethel was in her early sixties, and Alberta was fast approaching seventy.

Alberta had every hair in place and wore only the finest linens and silks. Ethel had a cut-and-curl and donned matching polyester.

Ethel was just plain ole folk. She was a widow who had farmed for years with her husband until he passed. Ethel had kept the farmhouse but leased the land to some youngsters trying to make a go of farming. She kept herself busy by working part time for Mary Ann, taking care of things in the front half of the store.

Alberta, on the other hand, had never stepped foot on a farm. It was beneath her. She was a priss with a capital "P." Alberta's husband had been a businessman in Maiden, running an upper-end clothing boutique.

Although most people thought Alberta was wealthy, both Livy and Ethel were suspicious. In their minds, there was no way Alberta would be working in a piddly little drugstore if she didn't need the money. Ethel used it to her advantage when the need arose to put Alberta in her place.

Livy liked Ethel a lot. She reminded her of herself. She was sweet, which Livy could definitely be. And, she was ornery, a skill Livy had perfected by the age of two. Ethel's favorite game was "What can we do next to piss Alberta off?" Livy liked that game a great deal.

Both Alberta and Ethel worked part time, mostly on different days. But two days a week, they overlapped, and those were the days that Livy lived for because one of the days was Saturday.

Among their differences, the one that really annoyed Alberta was the way Ethel cleaned the fountain at the end of the day. Alberta was the poster child for anal retentiveness. Ethel, on the other hand, was perfectly content as long as she could find what she wanted among the clutter. Alberta put every utensil in what she believed was its proper place. She scrubbed the sink with a toothbrush and swept until the straw in the broom was coming out.

Ethel, much to Alberta's dismay, would clean, but she would leave the utensils to dry on a tea towel on the counter. It drove Alberta crazy.

When Alberta opened following a day that Ethel had closed, she would announce her arrival with "Oh my God! Would you just look at this mess?" Then, she would head straight to the back of the store, cackling all the way like a hysterical chicken.

"Mary Ann," she would humph at Livy's mother, "did you see the mess Ethel left in the fountain? Did you? You have got to do something about this, Mary Ann. I mean what are your customers going to say when they see that fountain looking like a pigsty? The Health Inspector is going to close us down! It's a disgrace, a complete and total disgrace." Finally, she would stop to take a breath.

"I know, Alberta," Livy's mother patronized. "I've asked her to put the utensils away. She just gets busy. But I'll talk to her again. I'm sorry."

Alberta would reply with another humph and storm off.

Livy heard her mother droll on to her father about it on many occasions. One day, she asked Ethel why she continued to leave the utensils out when she knew it made Alberta so mad.

"Because it makes Alberta so mad," she answered.

Livy had to admit, it was a good reason.

Similarly to most other days, Alberta was on the warpath again. It was at least her sixth trip by the soda table to spy on Livy and her friends.

"Livy," she finally said, pursing her lips and glaring a hole through the girl, "Don't you think you should straighten and refill the greeting cards?"

"She can do it later," Ethel interjected from behind the fountain. "Leave her be."

Livy debated on whether she should get up or let Ethel fight the battle for her. In the end, she didn't want to be the latest reason for the testiness between the two. She told her friends she would catch up with them later to plan their evening out. Then she went and straightened the cards.

When she finished, she went behind the fountain to make herself a cream soda.

"Thanks for taking up for me," she told Ethel.

"That old cow wouldn't know what to do if she weren't belly aching about something," Ethel replied. "One day, I would love to spike her drink with some Milk of Magnesia. Then, she would be keeping herself busy in the bathroom instead of in everybody's business."

Alberta was famous for knowing everybody's business. She knew and told everyone who would listen about the latest happenings in town – most of which she found out by working in the drugstore.

She would look through the prescriptions to see who had what ailment and she would eavesdrop on those naive enough to talk about their lives while sipping a soda. Livy had been privy to some of the most intimate secrets in town because of her association with Alberta, whose favorite phrase in the English language was "Did you hear?"

Ethel apparently liked the Milk of Magnesia idea because she was deep in thought. "I have decided we should conduct an experiment," she announced to Livy.

"What kind of experiment," Livy asked.

"An experiment about Alberta's gossiping. Let's see how long it will take Alberta to spread a rumor around town and how long it will take to come back to me," Ethel schemed.

Ethel's thinking was that she would be able to track down the exact links in the chain of the town's rumor mill and wreak havoc on it from there on out. Ethel put her plan into action by making up a rumor and telling Livy within earshot of Alberta.

"Livy," Ethel said, risking one eye on Alberta to make sure she was listening, "you will never believe what happened to me last night."

"What?" the teenager asked, faking immense curiosity.

"Well, I got this phone call about eleven-thirty. I was dead asleep when the phone rang. It startled me so bad, I almost wet my pants."

Livy began laughing at the thought.

"Who was it Ethel and why were they calling so late?" she asked, playing along.

"Well, I don't know who it was, but he wanted to know if I wanted some company."

"What do you mean?" Livy innocently asked.

"Just what I said," Ethel replied, acting annoyed with the girl's question. "He talked in this deep whispery voice and said, 'How'd you like some company, Ethel?'"

"Oh my God! What did you do?"

By this time Alberta was slinking closer to the fountain, trying to pretend that she was dusting and not listening to every word Ethel was saying. Ethel winked at Livy.

"Well, I told him that it depended."

"Depended on what?"

"I told him it depended on whether he was fast enough to outrun the ornery bull I keep in my front yard, and the buckshot I keep in my shotgun. Then I said, 'If you still want to keep me company, just come on out here,' and I hung up."

"Ethel," Livy chuckled, "you are a hoot. Did you really do that?"

"I sure did, and guess what?"

"What?"

"I lay there all night by my lonesome. Hell, I just don't get why men are so intimidated by me."

Livy laughed out loud.

Alberta slipped behind the cigar case next to the fountain and began putting on her windbreaker.

"I have to run an errand," she told Ethel. Then she turned to Livy, "humphed," and pushed her aside on her way out the door.

"Okay," Ethel answered her. "Hurry back."

As soon as Alberta exited the store, Ethel turned to Livy.

"Okay, start counting, the race is on. Want to make a wager on how long it takes to get back to me?" she asked.

"Yeah," Livy answered. "I think it will make its way back here by Tuesday."

Ethel cackled with a devious look in her eye. "I say Monday." She looked amused. "I can't wait to see how the story ends up by the time I hear it again. I bet before it is over, there will be a name attached to the voice. I'm certain the story will include me inviting him over and having my way with him on the front porch while wearing my best flannel nighty." She clapped her hands.

"Oh, God." Livy frowned, trying to clear that horrid image from her brain. "Let's hope it doesn't go that far. You better stick your head out the door and see where she's headed if you want to find out who are the members of the rumor mill."

"Oh yeah." Ethel said, heading for the door. "I bet her first stop will be Ralph's. She can kill a whole lot of birds with one stone there."

Ethel stuck her head out the door.

"Ha!" she said looking back at the girl. "I told you so. Straight to Ralph's. That old biddy. What a gossiping hag!"

"Now, now, Ethel, calm down. Just think, when the rumor comes full circle, you'll have the most priceless piece of information going, the map to the gossip circuit," Livy proclaimed.

Ethel liked that. She pulled her head inside, turned around and smiled. "You're right! I can use it to my benefit and I know just how."

"How?" Livy asked.

"Just never you mind," she said, brushing her much younger counter part aside. "It's best if you stay in the dark. There are some things children just don't need to be a part of."

"Hey," Livy objected, resenting the child remark. "I am a grown woman, I can keep a secret."

"Sure, you can," Ethel replied. "Sure, you can."

Chapter Nine

The Demise of Old Pete

About twenty minutes later, Alberta made her way back into the store. She had a small apple in one hand and a pack of gum in the other.

"Alberta," Ethel inquired, "why did you go buy gum? We have gum right here."

"Our gum isn't fresh," Alberta lied. "I like the gum from Ralph's. He has a better wholesaler."

Ethel looked at Livy, raised one eyebrow and stuck out her neck like a chicken. "That's the sorriest excuse I've ever heard in my life," she whispered. "That old bag of bones lies like she makes limeades – shitty."

Livy giggled, clasping her hand over her mouth so Alberta wouldn't hear. "Well, it won't be…"

The front door swung wide open, and Lee Loot shoved his head through to announce that there was an arrest going on up the street at Doodle's Five and Dime.

Ethel, Alberta, and Livy all made a mad rush toward the door, pushing each other aside to try and be the first to witness the excitement. Livy won, barely sliding through the door before Alberta.

Lester was leaving Doodle's with Old Pete. His hands were cuffed behind his back, and Lester was kind of pushing, steadying, and holding Old Pete up while he shuffled to the curb.

"Oh my God," Livy said, half whispering, although she didn't know why because it wasn't like Lester or Old Pete was going to hear a half a block away. "Lester's arresting Old Pete! What in the world do you think he did?" she asked anyone who was listening.

"I don't know but I'm going to find out," Alberta said, marching up the street toward Doodle's.

Ethel thought out loud. "There's no telling, but it must have been something really bad," she said. "Mrs. Doodle would never have Old Pete arrested. She's the nicest woman on this block. She wouldn't hurt a fly. Old Pete must have just gone berserk or something. I can't just stand here. I'm going up there too!" She turned to Livy. "You stay here and man the front. I'll be back in a minute. You'd better tell your mom what's going on. She'll want to know."

Livy ran to the back of the store telling the story as she went. Barbara, the pharmacy assistant, and Lucy, the bookkeeper, met her at the back cash register.

"What are you talking about?" Barbara said, looking puzzled.

"Old Pete just got arrested at Doodle's Five and Dime," Lily repeated. "We saw Lester with him in handcuffs. Alberta and Ethel went up there to find out what is going on."

About that time, Livy's mom stuck her head through the glass window of the pharmacy.

"Lester arrested Old Pete?" she asked. "What for?"

"I don't knooowwww," Livy said rolling her eyes and feigning exhaustion from having to retell the story. "Alberta and Ethel went to find out. They aren't back yet. But Ethel said it had to be something really bad like Old Pete going crazy or something because she said Mrs. Doodle would never have Old Pete arrested because she is just too nice."

"Well, that's true," Mary Ann said. "Mrs. Doodle doesn't have a mean bone in her body."

"What if he killed her?!" Livy asked, exciting herself with the thought that the town would finally have some real news to tell.

"Get a grip, Livy," Mary Ann groaned. "Old Pete couldn't kill a cockroach. He's too feeble."

"It could happen," Livy pouted. "Maybe he pushed her and made her fall and hit her head and cracked open her skull or something like that!"

"For crying out loud, would you just stop? Everything's a drama with you. Get back up to the fountain. You have customers," her mom demanded.

"Geez, I was just trying to figure it out," the overly theatrical girl whined on her way back to the fountain. "Ethel's the one that said it had to be something really bad, not me. I get blamed for everything."

Livy waited on customers, trying not to think about the melee up the street. But as soon as she finished the last order, she ran back to the front door and poked her head out.

The curb on that end of the block was much higher than in front of the drugstore. There was a concrete step added to help people get up on the sidewalk. Lester had Old Pete to the curb, and it looked like he was trying to pick him up like a sack of potatoes. Lester lifted the fragile man from the sidewalk and set him back down onto the street.

Ethel and Alberta were standing in front of the Five and Dime, talking to Mrs. Doodle. She was wringing her hands.

"Well, I guess she's not dead," Livy almost felt bad. *"Maybe Old Pete tried something on her. Ewww, that's just gross,"* Livy shook the disturbing thought from her head. She then sat back down on the soda canisters waiting for Ethel and Alberta to get back to the store. When they finally did, they sauntered in acting as if nothing had happened.

"What in the blue blazes is going on?" Livy jumped up and squelched her impulse to ask them what had taken their tired old butts so long.

"Oh, nothing," Alberta said, waving Livy off with her freshly manicured hands.

"What do you mean nothing? Are you kidding? Something was going on or Old Pete wouldn't have gotten arrested!" Livy was more than perturbed that Alberta was being, well, Alberta.

Mary Ann, Barbara and Lucy all appeared from the back.

"What happened, Ethel?" Livy's mother asked.

"Mrs. Doodle had Old Pete arrested because he stole some scissors."

Mary Ann, Barbara and Lucy all gasped.

"What?" Lucy asked. "Why in the world would she have him arrested? We all have an unspoken rule around here."

"We take care of Old Pete," Barbara interrupted. "If he needed scissors, she should have let him have them," she furrowed her brow. "It's just not right. What has gotten into Mrs. Doodle?"

Ethel interrupted.

"Well, we asked her the same thing. She said that she was more than happy to let him have a pair of scissors. She said he came in Tuesday and took a pair."

"She's just now waiting to have him arrested?" Mary Ann asked confused.

"No," Ethel said.

"Then what?" she asked.

"Mrs. Doodle said he came into the store again on Thursday. She said he took a second pair of scissors."

"Two pair?" Mary Ann raised an eyebrow.

"No," Ethel replied.

"What then? What are you talking about Ethel?" The store's owner was obviously becoming frustrated.

"He came in again today and he tried to take another pair."

"What? That doesn't make sense," Barbara said.

"Well," Ethel said, getting frustrated herself, "if you'll let me finish I'll tell you. Today was the third day this week that Old Pete has taken scissors from the Five and Dime. Mrs. Doodle said she didn't mind him taking a pair of scissors if he needed them. And she said she wasn't even really worried about the second pair because she thought he may have lost the first ones. But, she said when he came in today and took another pair, that was just the last straw. She said he was just thieving to be thieving and that was plain wrong. And besides, now she's out of scissors."

Mary Ann, Barbara, and Lucy all looked at each other, shrugged and walked back to their respective posts.

Ethel went back to the fountain and Alberta to the jewelry counter. Livy sat down at a soda table, thoroughly disgusted that the only excitement the town had to offer was an arrest for stolen scissors.

"Blah." she said under her breath.

Chapter Ten

You Have To Get Over

*L*ivy sat at the soda table in thought while waiting for the next customer to arrive. *"This place sucks. I wish I lived somewhere bigger and more exciting."* But then, she realized that something special was taking place. This had to be the first time – at least in her lifetime – that both jail cells were at capacity. *"Two arrests in one day,"* she marveled.

It didn't even bother her that one of the prisoners was passed out and had no idea he was even in jail, and the other was so old he was probably grateful for the rest. It was indeed a day for the history books.

The phone rang and Livy went to the counter beside the cash register to answer it.

"Stephens' Drug Store," she said in her best professional voice.

Livy liked to try out different sophisticated voices when answering the phone. The current one was her, "I work for the President of the United States and can't be bothered," voice.

"Livy!" Stevy shrieked from the other end.

"What? What's the matter, Stevy?"

"Your grandmother just ran into my mother!"

"So," Livy answered, bewildered by her friend's hysterics.

"IN HER CAR!" came the very testy reply.

"Seriously? You mean she ran over your mother?! Is she dead?!" Livy screamed.

"No, stupid, she didn't run over her. She hit my mother's car with her car!" Stevy huffed, clearly annoyed.

"Oh, good gravy, Stevy. Are they alright?"

"They're both fine. But she creamed the crapola out of mom's car."

"Okay, calm down and tell me what happened."

It was at this very moment that Stevy's mother, Maureen, walked in. "Is your mom here?" she asked Livy.

"Hold on, Stevy, your mom's here. I'll call you back," Livy said, hanging up the phone.

"She's in the back, Mrs. Peters. Are you okay?"

"Yes, I'm fine and so is your grandmother – just a little fender bender. I better go let your mom know."

Livy followed Maureen Peters to the back of the store. The woman stopped at the window of the pharmacy booth and looked up at Livy's mom who was filling a prescription.

"Mary Ann, I'm so sorry, but I had a wreck with your mom. She's okay, but I wanted to let you know so you could check on her. I'm so, so, sorry."

"What happened?" Mary Ann asked.

"Well, I was just leaving town down by the little gas station and I saw her coming. I said to myself 'That's Mrs. Belle, I better pull over.' But then I thought, 'No, it will be okay, she's driving pretty slowly.' But of course, the moment she saw me she started heading my way, and before I knew it, Bam! She had sideswiped me. It's totally my fault, I knew better. Don't worry I'll pay for the damage."

"Maureen, it was not your fault," Mary Ann said, trying to reason with her. "My mother hit you. You're the third person in two months."

"I know Mary Ann, but everyone in town knows that if they see Mrs. Belle coming they have to pull over. I knew it and I just didn't do it. It's my fault."

"I have got to get that car away from her," Livy's mother shook her head, "before she really hurts someone."

THE DRUGSTORE

Everyone in town did know Livy's grandmother's driving habits – fast and left of center. Mrs. Belle was only four feet, ten inches and could barely see over the steering wheel. She wore thick silver cat-rimmed glasses and had a matching poof of silver hair. It was all anyone could see when the fast and furious little woman was behind the wheel.

It was a stroke of luck that she drove a very bright purple 1970 Ford Galaxy, which made it easy for others to spot her.

Although the sweet old lady was quickly approaching eighty, Livy's grandmother could run circles around people half her age. If it weren't for her silver hair, most wouldn't have known that she had eight decades under her belt.

"You say Mother is okay?" Mary Ann asked Maureen.

"Oh yeah, she got right back in her car and headed to the church to set up the flowers for tomorrow's service. She told me to come talk to you, she was too busy and was, especially now, running late. I told her, okay, and off she sped like a bat out of…oh well, I mean like Mrs. Belle," Maureen apologized.

"I don't know what to do with her. Since my dad can't drive anymore, she does everything, which means she is on the road twice as much as she should be. Something's got to give, but I don't know what. If I even mention that she needs to stop driving, she gives me a look like I'm going to hell. She's got enough clout with the man upstairs that I think she could send me there," Mary Ann said, shaking her head. "I'll think of something. I'm glad you're okay Maureen, just let me know what it cost to get the car repaired and we'll take care of it."

Mrs. Peters never did give Mary Ann a total of the damages. She still believed it was all her fault.

The phone rang again.

"Hello," Livy sultrily answered. "Stephens' Dru…"

Before Livy could even finish the Drug part, Stevy started screaming again.

"What happened? What did my mom say? I cannot believe your grandmother hit her. You all really need to do something about her. Everyone in town knows she shouldn't be driving and you all just…."

Livy cut her off mid-sentence.

"Hey, wait a minute. I'm not the one who hit your mom," she said defensively. "Why are you blowing your top at me? It's not my fault."

"Well, that was my mom she hit, and she could have been really hurt. You all need to do something about your granny," Stevy said more calmly.

"What would you have us do, Stevy?" Livy retorted. "I'll tell you what, I think you should go tell her that she can't drive anymore. But be warned, she's gonna' whop you upside the head with her purse."

Stevy was quiet and stayed that way so long Livy thought she had hung up.

"Are you still there?" Livy asked.

"Yeah," came the meek reply. "I'm sorry Livy. I was just worried about my mom. I know it's not your fault and I know Granny Belle didn't mean to hit her."

"It's okay. If it makes you feel any better, your mom was just fine and so is Granny. Your mom said she just took a chance that Granny wouldn't come over the center line at her car when she saw it." Livy laughed, although she tried not to.

Fortunately, Stevy followed suit.

"The problem is," Livy explained, "she always thinks the other cars are coming at her instead of the other way around. I've grabbed the wheel a million times to pull her back onto her side. She gets mad and tells me 'I know how to drive! I don't need some little teeny bopper showing me how it's done.'"

Stevy continued laughing.

"Call me later," Livy said. "We'll finish making our plans for tonight."

"Okay. See ya later."

Chapter Eleven

The Funeral Home

*L*ivy sat back down on one of the canisters and kicked her legs, daydreaming about her first date with Mitch. She hoped it would take place that night but doubted the boy would even give her the time of day.

Ethel walked by and looked at the girl. "Whatcha doin' just sittin' there?" she asked.

"I'm bored. There's nothing to do. Can I go see Michael?"

Ethel squinted at Livy as if she wanted to ask her something, but instead, she waved her hand. "Get on out of here, but don't be gone long. Alberta may have a full-blown conniption fit."

"I'll be back before she knows I'm gone. Tell her I'm in the bathroom if she asks." Livy giggled. "And if she checks, tell her I'm playing hide and seek."

Ethel just shook her head.

Michael was one of Livy's good friends, and he worked at Winters' Funeral Home. He was unbelievably funny and a tad bit effeminate.

Although Livy highly suspected he was gay, she never asked. She thought if he wanted her to know, he would tell her.

Aside from his sexual preferences, Michael was a quirky kind of kid. He had an affinity for the dead; hence, his weekend job as a host at the funeral home.

Livy walked down the street past the two empty stores next to the drugstore and then stopped in front of Fran's Grocery and Tag Agency. Fran was her Grandmother Belle's best friend. She was in her late seventies and still ran the store, although Livy wasn't sure how. It took the poor woman decades to type one tag certificate.

First, she would load the paper into her dusty typewriter. But then, she would pull it out and insert in again only to pull it out again incessantly until she finally managed to get it in evenly.

She would peck, stop, hunt the next letter, and peck again before moving her glasses down her nose to peer more closely at what she obviously wasn't able to see well. After all that, she would resume the pecking for a few strokes before moving her head closer to the typewriter and adjusting her glasses again.

Everybody in the community knew it would take the feeble clerk at least an hour to accomplish what should have only taken five minutes. Instead of waiting they would drop off their insurance verification and run their errands in order to give her time to finish.

Livy loved Ms. Fran's store. Although the sign said it was a grocery store, there weren't any groceries in it except for a few pieces of fruit that Ms. Fran kept in a non-working refrigerated produce case. Everyone knew that Ms. Fran actually bought the fruit at Ralph's Grocery. She marked it at what she paid for it, but no one ever bought it. Why the eccentric woman felt she needed to have it remained a mystery.

Ms. Fran's store did have lots of junk that had been there for decades. In fact, it could have doubled as a museum. That was one of the reasons Livy loved it so much. A person could get lost looking at all the strange and somewhat exotic wares.

"Hi, Ms. Fran," Livy said, peeking her head through the front door.

Ms. Fran was sitting behind her dusty desk knitting.

"Well, hello child," she said obviously happy for some company. "Where's your Granny Belle?"

"I'm not sure," Livy answered. "I think she's at the church. She hit Mrs. Peters in her car earlier but she's okay."

"Oh my, is Mrs. Peters okay too?

"They are both fine. Mrs. Peters didn't pull over when she saw Granny coming."

"Oh no, she should have known better than that," Ms. Fran tisked.

Livy nodded her head in agreement before sitting down on a dusty chair in front of Fran's desk. "Are you keeping your doors locked at home, Ms. Fran?"

"Only at night. Why?" the woman cocked her silver-haired head to one side.

"Because of the break-ins."

"What break-ins?" Ms. Fran sat upright in her chair with great surprise.

"You mean you haven't heard about the break-ins of the old – I mean senior citizens?" Livy tried to cover her faux pas of calling Ms. Fran's age group old. Then Livy too sat upright, not believing that the woman hadn't heard about the biggest news in years.

"Ms. Fran, everyone is talking about it. I can't believe you haven't heard." Livy cautioned her about the two women targeting the senior citizens. "It's not safe here. You need to lock your doors." She nodded as if she were very wise.

"Well, Honey," Ms. Fran said, wrinkling her forehead, "this is the first I've heard of it. Are you sure?"

"Yeah, I'm really sure. It has been in the paper, and they even tried to get into my Granny Stephens' house." Livy fingered a hot pink fuzzy pompom ball with google eyes, that sat on Ms. Fran's desk, as she remembered the close call her grandmother had. "They tell people they are having car trouble and ask to use their phone. Luckily, Granny Stephens wouldn't let them into her house. She told them she would make the call for them. As soon as she turned away, they left. That's when she realized she could have been in some serious trouble." Livy sighed and looked at Ms. Fran like she should really take her seriously.

"Well, I'll be, child. I will have to check into that. Nobody told me anything about it," she was shaking her head. "Surely, I'll be safe though. Nobody would be foolish enough to try and get me where I live," she reasoned.

Livy thought Ms. Fran might be right because she just lived three blocks up the street, directly past the First Baptist Church.

"Yeah, Lester could easily see your house from Harvey's or the police station," she agreed. "But, it's better to be safe than sorry. You should still lock your doors."

"Oh, I will, I sure will," Ms. Fran nodded.

Livy stopped thumbing the pompom creature and got up to leave. "I'm on my way to see Michael down at the funeral home. I guess I better get going."

"He's a little different, isn't he?" the woman looked at Livy, raising her brow.

The question peaked Livy's interest, knowing that Michael's type was about as foreign to the old folks as Pakistanis, so she played dumb.

"What do you mean, Ms. Fran?"

"Well, I'm not sure. I can't really put my finger on it," the geriatric woman pondered. "I think it's his feathery hair. I've never seen hair like that on a boy." She continued to search her brain. "I guess they are all wearing it longer these days, though," she finally acknowledged.

"Oh," Livy laughed, seeing that a possible homosexual was indeed so foreign that her mind couldn't get beyond a haircut. "Yeah, Michael does have pretty long hair," she finally agreed.

"Oh, it doesn't matter," Ms. Fran waved her hand and laughed. "I think he's a fine boy. We old fogies just aren't used to all these new styles you youngins wear."

Livy chuckled again too. "I better get going, Ms. Fran. I've got to get back to the store soon," she turned to leave before turning back to the woman again. "Oh, if my granny comes by, tell her I said 'Hi.'"

"I will," Ms. Fran said smiling. "I'll tell her for you. Bye now." She waved a dainty and age-spotted arm.

Livy left Ms. Fran's and continued down the street. She crossed to the next block, looking in all the store windows as she passed them. Winters' was almost at the very end of the street before the circle. Livy could see that there were only two cars parked out front. That meant there was probably no dead bodies inside. Livy sighed her relief.

The door chimed as she walked in, but the parlor was deserted. Livy stood a moment waiting for Michael to greet her. When he didn't, she stepped inside the office, but found it too, was deserted. She went back into the lobby before daring to go to the back where the caskets and embalming rooms were located.

"Michael?" Livy asked quietly.

No one replied, so Livy continued her journey passing the first of two viewing rooms. She hesitantly peered into it and happily saw it was empty. She assumed the second would be as well so she confidently strode by. However, out of the corner of her eye, she could see a body in an open casket.

At the same time, she did a double take. Michael jumped out from behind the door. He had both arms extended above his head like a mad ape and screamed "Arrrgh!!!"

Livy jumped back and screamed in return. She tried to turn and run, but her feet twisted around each other sending her tumbling to the ground, face first. She continued to scream until her brain computed that it was only Michael who had jumped out at her and not a dead Zombie person.

"You jerk!" Livy shrieked, as she rolled over to face the prankster. "I almost wet my pants! You stupid jerk! You fathead jerk!" She got up from the floor and started pummeling Michael with one of the shoes that had come off on her trip to the floor.

"Now, now, girlfriend," Michael sissy talked while trying to protect himself from her blows. "Calm down. You don't want to upset Mrs. Spivey, do you?"

"What are you talking about you, big jerk? Who's Mrs. Spivey?" Livy was incredulous.

Michael moved to the side of her and gestured into the viewing room. "There she is," he said pointing to the pale corpse.

"Oh God, Michael. Why do you do that to me? You know I hate dead people. They are so…

"Dead?" Michael asked.

"Gross," Livy answered.

"Oh, you're such a pansy. They are not gross. They're just like you and me. Only they don't breathe."

"You are just brilliant, Michael," Livy scoffed while looking over his shoulder at the very old lady in the coffin.

"I don't think I know her," Livy moved forward to take a closer look.

"Probably not," Michael answered. "She was homebound for the past ten years at least. She lived in that little, yellow house across from the park."

"Hey, that's near my Granny Stephens' house," Livy replied. "Wait a second," she paused to look again. "I do know her. When I was little, I used to see her on her porch. She would watch us play in my granny's front yard. She was real sweet."

"We picked her up late last night," Michael answered.

"I should go see my granny tonight," Livy said, thinking aloud. "I bet she's a little shook up having one of her neighbors die."

"You don't have a hot date with that muffin, Mitch?" Michael mocked while making smoochy kissy lips.

"Shut up," Livy retorted. "You know he hasn't asked me out yet. Besides, I'm not telling you anything. You're a jerk," Livy, remembered her anger and glared at him.

"Oh, girl, you should get over it. I was just having a little fun with you." Michael, dismissed her.

"That was not fun." Livy pouted and looked back into the room. "And I kinda feel bad for screaming in front of Mrs. Spivey."

Michael laughed. "Oh, I'm sure it's okay; she's a little hard of hearing these days."

Livy rolled her eyes. "You are one sick puppy, Michael – one sick puppy."

"Only if I can be a poodle," he said, smiling. "I just love poodles, don't you?"

Livy shook her head and turned to leave, not giving her charismatic friend the satisfaction of an answer.

"Bye, Michael."

"Byyyyye," he sang.

Chapter Twelve

The Great Mystery

As soon as Livy got back to the drugstore, she called her Granny Stephens.

"Hello?" her grandmother answered.

"Hi Granny, it's Livy. I heard about Mrs. Spivey, are you okay?"

"Well, of course, I'm okay. Why wouldn't I be?" the spry woman asked.

"Well, I just wanted to make sure, seeing that she's your neighbor and all. I thought you might be upset," Livy explained.

"Honey, at my age if I got upset every time one of my neighbors died, I'd be in a permanent state of depression."

Livy decided she had a point. Her grandmother, at seventy-four, was the baby of her street as most of the neighbors were well into their eighties. Livy knew that in the past year alone, two others had died, and one had gone into a nursing home. It was something Livy didn't want to think about for the woman who had helped raise her.

However, the subject of a nursing home had come up a lot recently, although Livy wasn't sure why. She had assumed that most old folks didn't want to talk about nursing homes much less be taken to one, but Maude Stephens didn't seem to have that aversion. Livy wondered if it was because she was lonely. All five of the woman's grandchildren were next to grown and didn't need her to babysit them anymore. Also, their visits had become fewer and farther between because some had left for college and the others had busy school lives. The thought made Livy sad.

Mrs. Stephens must have been thinking about it too because she reminded Livy of her wishes again.

"You remember," she relayed, "that if I ever have to go into a nursing home I want to go to Bentley's in Maiden – not Tinsley's," she asserted. "My friend Vera got to go to Bentley's last winter, and she loved it. She said she had the time of her life. All they did was play games and eat. That's my kind of party."

"Granny, you are never going to a nursing home. I will take care of you," Livy countered.

"Child, you can't even take care of yourself. How are you going to deal with a drooling old woman who's half out of her head?"

"You do not drool, Granny," Livy replied.

"Not yet anyway," the woman sassed. "I'm just saying I don't want to stay at Tinsley's. I want Bentley's. My friend Vera says she is thinking about breaking her hip just so she can go back."

"Granny, why don't you and Vera get together and keep each other company? You can have your own party. She just lives across the street." Livy tried to reason with the woman.

"She can't see well enough to cross the street," Livy's grandmother replied. "Besides, you can't have a party with just two people. We need lots of people – boys and girls."

"Granny!" Livy was shocked that the sweet little old woman even thought about men.

"What?" Mrs. Stephens innocently responded. "Just because there's snow on the rooftop don't mean there ain't a fire in the furnace," she giggled.

Now horrified, Livy scolded, "Granny, stop! "You should not be talking like that!"

"Oh boy, have you got a lot to learn youngin'," the saucy lady laughed again. She changed her thought mid-stream "Hey, have you had your very first kiss yet?" she sheepishly inquired.

"Yeah, in fifth grade," Livy droned, trying to sound much more mature than she actually was.

"Oh fiddle, that's not a real kiss," her grandmother retorted. "A fifth grader doesn't even know to change their underpants every day much less give a boy a proper kiss."

Livy blushed and changed the subject.

"Granny, are you keeping your door locked?" she quizzed. "I don't want those women coming back to your house and getting in this time."

"Don't you worry about me, I may be old but I can still whack someone with a broom," the woman boasted.

Even though she acted tough, Livy knew she had been frightened. When Livy last had visited, she noticed that her grandmother was, in fact, keeping a broom by her door and a large metal flashlight on her nightstand. Livy was heartbroken because she realized that for the first time in her life, her granny was scared to be living alone. It just wasn't right.

"How did you find out about Mrs. Spivey?" her grandmother asked, snapping her back to their conversation.

"I visited my friend Michael at the funeral home. He works there. "Granny, I've got to go. I'm at work and mom doesn't like me tying up the phone."

"Okay honey, but I wanted to tell you something before you go. Last night, when they were taking Mrs. Spivey away, I would have sworn that I saw one of the ladies that tried to use my phone that day."

"One of the ladies that you thought was going to rob you?" Livy asked, astonished.

"Yes. There was no girl with her though, just that police man and another man who drove the hearse."

"Are you sure, Granny?"

"Well no, not exactly. It was pretty dark, but they were under the street lamp in front of Mrs. Spivey's. It sure looked like her. She was real heavy with that bad bleached blonde hair and roots so wide she looked like an inverted skunk."

Livy chuckled at her grandmother's creative description but quickly refocused on the startling issue. "Granny, you make sure and keep your door locked," she warned her again. "I'll check into that woman and see what I can find out. I know they haven't caught her yet. Lester the policeman said they still don't have any good leads," she relayed what she had overheard that morning from the coffee gang. "He's brought in some Oklahoma City police or investigators or something like that to help him. I'm glad you're okay. I'll check on you tomorrow, okay?"

"That'll be just fine," her grandmother answered.

"Bye, Granny. I love you," Livy felt a tear coming into her eye. She would die if anything bad happened to the woman who was more like a mother than a grandmother.

"Love you too, Sweetie."

Livy composed herself as she hung up the phone. Then, she put her brain to work trying to figure out how she could find out about the woman her grandmother thought she had seen.

She picked up the phone again and dialed the funeral home.

"Winters' Funeral Home," Michael said in a very professional yet prissy voice.

"Michael, did you help pick up Mrs. Spivey last night?" Livy asked.

"Nope, Richy was on last night, why?"

"Does Richy normally pick up the people?"

"It depends on if he's working or not. Why?"

"Well does Richy have a girlfriend?" Livy continued the query.

"Not that I know of. Why?"

"Well then, who else would be with him to pick up a dead person?" Livy wondered aloud.

"No one. WHY?" Michael was obviously agitated with Livy for not answering his whys.

"So, does Richy or whoever picks up the body always go completely by themselves?" Livy continued to ignore his question.

"No, the police will usually come too. They make sure there is nothing suspicious. Why?!" Michael demanded yet again.

"So, you're telling me that Lester will also go? Who else?" Livy ignored Michael's hostile tone.

"Livy, so help me, I will not answer another single question out of your mouth until you tell me WHY!" he yelled, causing Livy to pull the phone away from her now ringing ear.

"Okay, calm down," she huffed, now agitated herself. "My granny said that there was a woman at Mrs. Spivey's last night when they picked her up."

"So?!" Michael loudly exhaled, exasperated that Livy still refused him. "What's the big deal about a woman? It was probably Mrs. Spivey's daughter or something," he negated.

"I don't think so," Livy's voice trailed off and Michael could tell she was not talking to him, but clearly thinking aloud again.

"Livy, you drive me crazy! Just tell me why you care if there was a woman there?"

"Because, Oh Impatient One" she chastised, "my grandma thinks she saw the woman who was going to rob her over at Mrs. Spivey's. Do you think the woman could have robbed Mrs. Spivey and killed her?" Livy asked, becoming enamored with her own sleuthing."

"No." he answered.

"Why not? I mean, if that was the woman, and she was there, and Mrs. Spivey is old like everyone else that got robbed, then it just makes sense that she was robbed too. And maybe Mrs. Spivey fought back or had a gun or a knife or something and tried to kill the robber. And maybe the robber had to kill her first," Livy thought she was getting really good at being a detective.

"Nice scenario Livy, but she died of a heart attack."

"Well, there you have it!" Livy said, slamming her hand onto the counter. "She was so scared of the robber that she died of a heart attack! We need to call the police, Michael! We should call the FBI or FBA or whatever that thing that investigates stuff like this is called!"

"I wouldn't do that if I were you, Livy," Michael, lisped.

"Why not? We could be heroes," she dreamed. "We can solve a case that no one else has been able to solve," Livy did not understand why Michael was trying to rain on her detective's parade.

"First of all, Mrs. Spivey had the heart attack two days earlier. When they found out she wasn't going to make it, her family wanted to take her home to die. It was her wish. Secondly, her family was with her when she died. So, if there was a robber, she would have had to rob everyone there. I don't think she would have been able to pull that off." Livy could feel Michael rolling his smug eyes.

"Are you sure?" she asked, knowing that her theory had just gone up in smoke.

"Yeah, I'm sure. I work here, don't I?"

"Well then, who was that woman?" Livy demanded again.

"I have no idea," Michael replied. "But if it will make you feel any better, I'll ask Richy if he took anyone with him."

"Yeah, that's a great idea," Livy slapped her hand on the counter again. "Do that and call me back, okay?

"Oh yes, My Queen," he sarcastically replied. "Anything for Your Highness."

"Whatever!" Livy rolled her eyes. "Call me back." She hung up the phone, dreaming of the excitement that could be awaiting her.

Chapter Thirteen

The Rumor Makes Its Rounds

Not more than one hour had passed since Alberta went on her blabbing spree when Tootsie Wilder came through the door wagging her lips. Tootsie was nearly as big of a gossip as Alberta.

"Oh, Ethel?" Tootsie sang in her "I know something you don't know," voice.

Ethel was standing behind the jewelry counter, and Tootsie walked right past, not seeing her. Ethel put her finger to her lips to tell Livy not to say anything, and then she ducked behind the counter.

"Ethel's ugh…not in sight right now," Livy said, trying not to lie yet again.

"Well," Tootsie began as if she were exasperated, "what's this I hear about Ethel's new boyfriend?"

Livy pretended to be completely surprised and know nothing about a boyfriend. "A what?" she answered. "Ethel has a boyfriend?"

"Oh, yes." Tootsie became wide eyed and ecstatic that she had fresh ears in which to plant her seed. "Ethel has a new male companion. He comes to see her at the farm..." she started looking around to make sure no one was overhearing, then she leaned over the counter, cupped her hand over her mouth so any eavesdroppers in the completely deserted store, couldn't hear what she was saying. "He comes over late at night and they... well, you know." Tootsie slyly giggled.

"No," Livy responded, leading her all the way to slaughter. "They do what?" she asked as innocently as her face would let her.

"Oh, I shouldn't be telling you this," Tootsie continued in her fake whisper. "After all, you are still pretty young. You probably don't know about these things."

"What things?" Livy asked, playing along.

"The birds and the bees, of course," Tootsie said, still looking around for any busybodies other than herself.

"Ohhhh, that!" Livy laughed. "Of course, I know about the birds and the bees. I'm fifteen. I've known about that stuff for a long time," she said, trying to show off her maturity.

"Well in that case," Tootsie said, more excited than ever. "Ethel and her boyfriend stay up all night having wild sex. They sometimes even do it on the porch!" She giggled and actually turned a little pink in the cheeks.

"You have got to be kidding?" Livy countered, falsely astonished. "Ethel? That doesn't sound like Ethel. She's never mentioned a boyfriend to me. Who is he?"

"Well, I'm not supposed to tell, but I guess it's okay considering how well you know her and everything. It's Festus Marney. That's why he comes in here every day. He acts like he wants to talk shop with the boys, but he's really here to see Ethel. I'd keep my eye on them two if I were you. Don't go letting them sneak to the back together, if you know what I mean." Tootsie raised her eyebrows.

Livy was about to come apart laughing but managed to keep her composure.

"Okay," she said, nodding in agreement, as if she would obey. "I'll make sure they don't go off together. Boy, I just can't believe it. Ethel has a boyfriend," Livy shook her head dramatically.

"And a questionable one at that!" Tootsie exclaimed.

Quite to the contrary, Festus Marney was far from wild. He was a retired mechanic who had served in World War II.

He had taken some shrapnel to the face, which left him slightly disfigured. His mouth looked like it had been burned, and he sometimes drooled a little from one side when he drank his coffee. The only other evidence of war wounds showed in his eyes. They were dark pools that held the pain of stories never told and times wished never to be relived.

"What do you mean questionable, Mrs. Wilder?" Livy, being fond of the man, came to his defense. "Mr. Marney has always seemed pretty quiet to me," she disagreed.

"Oh, well, he may seem that way," Tootsie brushed her off, "but I've heard that as soon as the sun goes down, he is at the bar livin' it up." She cocked her head sideways, seeing if Livy was now buying into the tale.

"Well, I'll be," Livy feigned. "I guess you just don't really know some people, do you?"

"That sure is the truth," Tootsie agreed, as she readied herself to leave. "Well, I must be getting on home. Herman will want some lunch, and I swear he can't fix a cracker for himself."

"Okay. Well, you have a good day, Mrs. Wilder," Livy lightly waved.

"Oh, I will," she said. "Oh, and don't tell Ethel I told you about her boyfriend. She might misunderstand and think I was gossiping or something. I just hate gossips. Don't you?"

"Yes, I would have to say I do," Livy answered sarcastically. "I would have to say I do."

Chapter Fourteen

Bob

*E*thel jumped up from behind the jewelry counter. "Well that old Biddy! Misunderstand her gossiping? Did she really just say she didn't want me to misunderstand and think she was gossiping?" Ethel crowed in disbelief.

"That's what she said," Livy replied through her laughter. "So, we were both wrong, it wasn't Monday, and it wasn't Tuesday. The rumor made it back here in fifty-seven minutes flat. What are you going to do now?" Livy asked the seething woman.

"I am going to track down the underground gossiping railroad," Ethel retorted, "and I'm going to do it right now."

Ethel grabbed her jacket and headed out the door on her way to Ralph's. Livy shrugged her shoulders and sat down to wait for the outcome. She spied Alberta coming back to the fountain after her rest break as she called it. Livy surmised that if there was ever a time for Alberta to stay on a break, it was then, but she wasn't about to warn the disagreeable clerk.

"Where is Ethel?" Alberta demanded as soon as she made it to the fountain.

"She had to run an errand," Livy could barely contain herself enough to arrest the smile that wanted to cross her face.

"When is she coming back?" Alberta demanded again.

"I don't really know," Livy answered. She tried to remain nonchalant while knowing that all hell was about to break loose.

Alberta started in on one of her many tirades. "I swear that woman is always leaving this fountain filthy. One of these days that health inspector will walk in here and then before we can say 'diddly doo,' he will shut us right down," she ranted.

Livy sat silently trying not to smirk or roll her eyes, but it wasn't long before her need to antagonize got the best of her.

"Alberta, you could eat off this floor, and the counters are gleaming. Just what around here is so dirty that it would make the health inspector shut us down?" Livy challenged her nemesis.

Alberta whipped around to face the teenager, steam coming from every visible orifice. "You must be blind!" she hissed, poking Livy in the chest. "Have you seen under this grate lately? Well? Have you?"

"Not since this morning when I swept it," Livy smugly rebutted.

"Well just you look here," she said pointing to a tiny piece of a potato chip. "Do you see that? Well? Do you?"

Livy followed Alberta's pointing finger. "You mean that piece of potato chip?" she said, smirking, unable to believe that the small little crumb was the only reason for the most recent of Alberta's spaz fits.

"Yes, that's exactly what I mean." Alberta put her hands on her hips. "It's absolutely," she slowly spilled out the word for added emphasis, "disgraceful how Ethel leaves this place! I swear she is going to be the death of me! She may like to work in a pigsty; after all, I guess she's right at home considering she was a pig farmer, but I want to work someplace clean." Alberta showed no signs of slowing down. "My home is clean, my car is clean, and by God, my work area is going to be clean!"

Livy went all out to defend Ethel's honor. "Alberta, Ethel was not a pig farmer. She was a regular farmer – you know, corn, okra, beans, that kind of thing."

"Oh poo!" Alberta brushed the girl away with a flip of her wrist. "I don't care if she farmed kumquats using armadillo droppings. She likes filth. I would hate to see her house. I bet it just plain stinks. I bet she has cockroaches!"

It was obvious to Livy that Alberta was on a tirade that could not be stopped. Seeing she was having no effect other than keeping it going, Livy let it slide.

"Nasty, nasty, nasty. I never in my life saw anyone so nasty," Alberta continued, mumbling under her breath.

Livy shrugged and picked up a comic book before sitting back down.

"I wonder just who she thinks she is," Alberta continued her rant while Livy ignored her. "I clean and clean and clean. And what does she do?" Alberta paused for a deep breath. "Nothing but mess things up. I swear I don't know how..."

About that time, Bob Cutter came into the store. Bob was a middle-aged and balding traveling salesman and when he came into the store, it was his mission to rile Livy and her younger brother, Sam. Livy sunk down onto the canister, trying to keep the verbal assailant from seeing her. It didn't work.

"Well hello, ladies!" he shouted.

"Hello, Mr. Cutter," Livy begrudgingly answered.

"Hello, Bob," Alberta said.

"Say there, cheerleader girl," he pointed to Livy. "I heard you have the hots for the quarterback," he taunted. "You better grow some bigger produce up there if you want to attract popular boys like that." He pointed to Livy's chest. "You and your giggly little entourage don't have a chance with those high school football players unless you think they like girls who still carry around their blankies and bottles" he guffawed.

Livy gritted her teeth, at the same time wondering how he had heard and trying to keep from saying something she would regret to the mean-spirited man. It irritated her to the core that she could never think of a quick or witty comeback. Each time he came into the store, he would scorch her, and leave her to sizzle with no repercussions. Livy wished that just once she could think of something that would shut the man up, but it appeared this day was not going to be the one.

Once Bob could see he was getting a rise out of her, he continued his provocation.

"So, where's that Polack brother of yours? Did you hear about the nickname I gave him?" he asked the girl.

When Livy refused to answer, he directed the question to Alberta.

"Alberta, do you know what I call her little brother?" he asked, laughing at his own joke before he told it.

"I don't think I do Bob. What are you calling him these days?" Alberta asked with a smile. She liked Bob because he badgered both Livy and Sam, who she thought were nothing but spoiled brats.

"I call him CATFISH!" Bob laughed from the deepest part of his belly. "You know...har...ha...why I...hee hee hee...call...hahaha...him...oh Lordy, that's funny," he said holding his gut, "Catfish?"

"You must tell Bob, you must tell," Alberta faked a laugh of her own.

"Because he's all mouth and no brains! Ha ha ha...get it? All mouth and no brains?" Bob slapped his thigh.

"Oh, my!" Alberta momentarily pretended to be taken aback in case Livy's mother was watching. But as soon as she realized that she wasn't, she let out a real laugh, but put her hand to one side of her mouth to cover the view from Mary Ann. "Oh, that's clever. That was a good one," she laughed.

Livy pursed her lips and put her hands on her hips. "You better not let my brother hear you say that," she challenged.

"Why not?" Bob smirked. "He may talk a mean streak but he don't have nuthin' to back it up with. Like I said, he's all mouth! Ha ha ha."

"He may only be fourteen, but he can be very mean when he wants to," Livy said straightening her shoulders and jutting out her jaw to look confident.

"Oh Lordy!" Bob laughed hysterically again. "Oh Lordy, Alberta, did you hear that? Her bubba can be really mean!" He turned back to Livy. "Oooh, I'm shakin' in my boots, cheerleader girl! Shakin' in my boots." He scoffed at her before walking toward the back of the store, chuckling and snickering all the way. Livy assumed he was going to get some Pepto-Bismol for his chronic condition of diarrhea of the mouth.

She then turned to Alberta. "That was not funny, Alberta."

Alberta smirked. "Oh yes, it was."

"You wait til I tell my mom," Livy threatened.

"Your mother will think it was funny too," she said, waving the girl off.

"You sad, old bat," Livy hissed under her breath.

"What?" Alberta swung around challenging the teen.

Livy, who knew better than to disrespect her mother's employees, glared at Alberta again, before answering. "Nothing," she huffed.

Alberta set her eyes and then grinned. "That's what I thought you said."

Livy walked away and went behind the jewelry counter to lick her wounds.

There, she sat fuming over the sewage that had been unleashed on her. She decided that Alberta had just become number two on her shit list, right behind Bob. Little did Alberta know, but that wasn't good news for her.

Chapter Fifteen

Lunch

*L*ivy was still steaming when Ethel came back into the store. Alberta had gone to the back to check in stock. Livy returned to the coke canister to continue her pouting.

Ethel asked the sullen girl. "What's the matter?"

"Butthole Bob is here," Livy hissed. "He was making fun of me and Sam."

"Sam and me," Ethel corrected. "Don't let him get to you, Livy. The more you let it affect you, the more he's gonna do it."

"I hate his ugly, stinkin' guts," she replied.

"Well, if you'll just ignore him, he'll leave you alone. He only messes with you because he gets such a rise out of you," Ethel reiterated.

"Easier said than done," Livy countered. "Next time he sticks his fat face in mine and starts in, I swear to God, I'm going to grab those nose hairs that are always stickin' out and yank em out," she growled.

"Take a walk, girl. You need to cool down. Get out of here for a while," Ethel suggested.

"Fine," Livy got up from her seat. "I'm going to Ralph's for a sandwich. Do you want one?"

"No," Ethel replied, "but I need you to go to the bank and get some one-dollar bills. We're almost out," she said, handing the girl two twenties.

The First National Bank was two stores up from Ralph's, right next to Doodle's Five and Dime. When Livy was small, her grandfather repeatedly told her the story of how Pretty Boy Floyd and an accomplice by the name of George Birdwell had robbed it in 1931.

Mr. Belle told her the two pulled up to the bank in broad daylight, not even attempting to hide who they were. He said that Pretty Boy and Birdwell got out of the car, walked into the bank, and demanded all the money. He always seemed amazed when he revealed that the bank president gave them the twenty-five hundred dollars before they left with no trouble.

The thing that had impressed her grandfather the most, however, was the way in which Pretty Boy was dressed. Mr. Belle had described in great detail the beautiful black, pinstriped suit and silk burgundy tie the criminal had worn.

"He was really impressive," her grandfather would say with a gleam in his eye.

When Livy had exchanged the money, she walked back down to Ralph's. Ralph's store was pretty small, a lot smaller than Pendleton's, which was directly across the street. Livy made her way back to the meat counter, saying hello to Betsy, the checkout lady, and then to Ralph.

"Heard your grandmother was in another wreck this morning," Ralph said.

Livy acknowledged the incident. "Yeah, she ran into Mrs. Peters. But they're both okay."

Ralph shook his head and laughed. "That Mrs. Belle. She is hell on wheels."

Livy had to agree. "That she is," she smiled, almost proud of the fact.

Livy headed to the back of the store to the deli.

The butcher was Morty. He was a small fellow with slicked, black hair that was poofed to look like Elvis. Livy looked into the meat case at the different cold cuts before deciding upon the olive loaf.

"Can I get an olive loaf with mayonnaise," she smiled at the man.

"You sure can," Morty answered. "What ya up to today, youngin?"

Livy rolled her eyes in fake disgust. "Just working for my mom."

Morty admonished her. "Now, you are learning a good lesson working for your mom," he imparted. "It teaches you the value of hard work."

"I'm learning a lot of things," Livy replied. "But most of them wouldn't fall into that category."

Morty stared at her blankly, not catching on to her sarcasm. "Well, you do a good job for your mom and maybe someday, you'll own her store," he said, passing her the sandwich wrapped in white paper.

"I'd rather inherit lice," Livy wanted to say, but instead answered with "thanks."

Livy took her sandwich to the front and asked Betsy to put it on her mother's bill. As she was leaving the store, Ralph stopped her. He stood there a moment weighing his words before speaking.

"I was debating on whether to say something, but I really think I should," he said with a sort of grimace.

"What's the matter?" Livy asked him.

"Well, now don't get me wrong. I don't want to tell your momma how to run her business, but I just feel like I've got to say something, especially after today," he said looking around to make sure no one was close by and listening. "I've been having a little problem with your mom's clerk Alberta, and I wondered if she might have a talk with her."

Livy's dramatic imagination kicked into overdrive. "She's not stealing from you, is she?"

"Oh, no, no," Ralph shook his head. "She's not stealing – it's nothing like that. It's just that she likes to come up here and gossip about people," he imparted. "Most of the time, it's not a problem. She might just catch somebody in the aisle and give them the lowdown. But recently, she's kind of got a band of groupies." He sighed.

Livy couldn't wait for Ralph to tell her more.

"They come in here Saturday mornings, and they wait for Alberta to show up. They clog up my aisles and make it hard for the other customers to get around. And today, oh Lord, today was over the top." Ralph sighed again.

"What happened?" Livy anxiously asked, realizing she might just be on the verge of busting open the underground gossip railroad and relishing in how proud Ethel would be.

"Well, she came in this morning and she kind of held court. It was the craziest thing I've ever seen," he declared. "As soon as she walked in the door, her groupies surrounded her. She was waving her hands and saying, 'Oh! You are not going to believe this! You are not going to believe it!'"

Ralph continued with his story, explaining how the women kept asking Alberta to speak up, until finally she went to the checkout counter, grabbed the microphone, and broadcasted to the entire store that Ethel was having an affair.

"I had to go and wrestle the microphone away from her, but by the time I did, it was too late. Poor Ethel," he said while wiping his brow with a hankie. "I just don't know what to do. Do you think you could tell your mom about it and let her handle it?"

"I'll tell her but I don't know if she'll do anything," Livy shrugged. "I think she's kind of afraid of Alberta."

Ralph grimaced "Oh well, I can't blame her there," he agreed. "I think I'm a little afraid of her too. That tongue of hers could do some real damage to someone, just like poor Ethel."

Livy thought for a moment. "Don't worry about Ethel," she said, beginning to smile. "Ethel knows how to handle Alberta. Anyway, I'm sorry for everything. I will tell my mom and let you know what she does. See ya later, Ralph."

"See ya, little un," he said.

Chapter Sixteen

Hell Hath No Fury

*L*ivy sprinted back to the drugstore thinking that it was about to be the best day of her life. After Alberta's earlier meanness, she could not wait for payback. She blew through the front door, but before she could start any trouble, she ran straight into the Bendys who were standing at the fountain.

The four Bendys, with their dirty faces and their greasy, blond hair were the meanest kids around. They lived to beat up any unsuspecting child who was unaware that they should never walk past the Bendy house alone. Livy hated them. No, she abhorred them. Yet there they were, right in the store at the worst possible time.

Livy made her way around them to get behind the fountain, glaring at the two oldest girls with all the hate she could muster. The two had stolen the most prized possessions that Sam and she had owned, the ten-speed bikes they'd gotten for Christmas two years earlier.

Livy and Sam had only had the bikes a few months and were riding them in town at her Grandmother Belle's house. The two parked the bikes in her grandmother's driveway to go inside and get a drink. But, as soon as they had gotten off and started to walk inside, the Bendys came around the corner in an old pickup truck, jumped out, and grabbed the bikes. They sped off laughing and taunting the pair.

Sam pursued them at a full run, but he was no match for the pickup. When he came to the realization that there was no hope of catching them, he crumpled to the street and started to cry.

"Those sons of bitches," he yelled. "They stole our bikes!"

Sam was obsessive about his bike because as he was the last of five kids; it was the first one he ever had that wasn't a hand-me-down or some shade of pink passed down from one of his three older sisters. "I don't believe it," he wailed, continuing to sit, head in hands.

"It's okay Sam, we'll get them back," Livy consoled while helping him up. "Come on, let's go call Mom."

The two did call Mary Ann, who in turn called Lester and made him come to the store. She told him that the Bendy girls took the bikes. Lester walked out the back of the drugstore and over to their house, which was located across the alleyway. When he got to their place, there was no sign of the girls or the bikes, so Lester informed Mary Ann there was nothing he could do until they got home.

"Can't you put out an APB or something, Lester?" she demanded.

"I could put out an APB," Lester replied, "But I would be the only one to see it. Besides, we have to determine that there was really a crime," he reasoned.

"Great jumping Jehoshaphat!" Livy's mother exploded. "That is the most screwed up thing I have ever heard. You know those Bendys are trouble. They always have been. And besides, I am telling you there was a crime, Lester!" she fumed. It also wasn't lost on her that she had shelled out sixty-five bucks each on the bikes.

Lester tried to reason with her. "Well now Mrs. Stephens, we gots to have some proof."

"Proof?!" the irate woman yelled. "You don't need any proof. My kids saw them take the bikes. What more proof do you need than that?" Mary Ann put her hands on her hips, challenging Lester to argue with her.

Lester tried to placate the pharmacist by proposing that sometimes kids make things up to get other kids in trouble, but he only managed to increase her aggravation.

"Oh yeah, my kids, who live on their bikes, are going to hide them and not ride them just to get the Bendys in trouble. Come on Lester," she spat before sending out a warning. "You better get them Lester or I will. And I promise you, you do not want me taking care of the Bendys."

Livy's mother rarely cussed, but this was one of the exceptions. "I will make those little bastards lives' hell – I swear it, so you damn sure better get to them before I do."

Lester tried to calm the normally agreeable woman. "Now, now Mrs. Stephens, You shouldn't talk like that. You would feel real bad if something happened to one of them, and you said something like that."

"The hell I will," Mary Ann huffed.

Lester waved an arm, as if fanning her "Ms. Stephens, just calm down. You have my word I will investigate this completely. If those Bendy kids stole your youngins' bikes, I will find it out. Don't you worry."

The Bendy Bike Caper went much like the Senior Citizen Crime spree – unsolved. Livy and Sam never saw the return of their favorite mode of transportation, although they had spotted the Bendy girls on the bikes just a few weeks later. Again, by the time they got Lester on it, the bikes were nowhere to be found. So the next Christmas, Mary Ann gave up and replaced the stolen ones.

Livy sat down on the soda canister and never took her enraged eyes off them. Usually, if there was more than one customer, she would have jumped in to help the other clerks. However, there was no way she was going to wait on the thieves. Ethel, who was aware of the event, knew of Livy's hostility and wasn't about to ask her to help. But an unsympathetic Alberta, wanted to torment Livy even more. She made a very big mistake.

"You need to get up and help these customers," she snidely remarked as she walked past the girl.

Livy clenched her teeth. "Leave me alone, Alberta."

Alberta wasn't going to back down and instead stepped up onto her soapbox. "You have been gone all morning long, and the time you have been here, you have been sitting around gossiping with your little friends. Your momma pays you to work, not sit around on your duff and play all day," she chided.

Livy had all of Alberta's crap she was going to take – Bendys or not. She took one big breath and then unleashed on the meddler. "At least, I don't sit around gossiping all day! What about you, Alberta? I didn't go up to Ralph's and announce over the microphone that Ethel is having an affair with Festus Marney!" the girl yelled.

Ethel's head snapped to look at Livy and then back to Alberta.

"What's that all about, Alberta?" Livy knew she finally had the perfect ammunition with which to lambast the unsuspecting gossip, and thus, continued her condemnation. "In fact," she sneered, "you want to tell Ethel what you've been saying about her or do you want me to do it?!" Livy donned an evil and smug smile on her face.

Mary Ann, Barbara and Lucy all peered out of their holes trying to see why Livy was yelling.

"That's right Alberta, I know all about it," Livy continued her Alberta induced eruption. "You talk about me traipsing up and down the street," she scoffed pointing her finger at the now uncertain antagonist. "I understand you do it every single Saturday just so you can spread your nasty rumors about people!"

Livy was now on a full-blown high horse, but at the same time, she could feel her face growing hot, signaling she was about to cry. It was something Livy hated about when she got angry because it took away all her intimidation. She took a breath to get a hold of herself and to keep her tears at bay. She firmly set her jaw so that she would not give the Bendys or Alberta the satisfaction of seeing her cry.

When she finally regained her composure, she swung around to face Ethel.

"Guess what Ethel? There is no gossiping underground railroad," she pointed to the now silent Alberta. "It's her and only her! She goes to Ralph's every week and announces all her gossip. Today, she even got on Ralph's microphone and told everyone in the store that you are having an affair with Festus Marney!" Livy became smugger by the minute.

At the same time, it was apparent that Ethel was becoming madder, her face reddening to a shade of dark raspberries. Alberta began to slink away.

Livy wasn't about to let Alberta get away and continued to mock her. "Where're you going Alberta?" she taunted, as the woman moved to take refuge behind the jewelry counter. "Don't you want to tell Ethel all about her affair since you know so much about it?"

Now safe behind the jewelry counter, Alberta found her voice. "You need to hush your mouth!" she hissed at the girl.

Ethel pushed past Livy, and into the aisle that separated the fountain from Alberta.

"No Alberta," she seethed, "I think you are the one who needs to hush your mouth," Ethel warned. "I have had it up to here with you and your damn gossiping." Ethel gestured to her neck. "You are constantly trying to make trouble for me, and I am sick of it!"

The Bendys, who had remained to witness the standoff, grabbed their ice cream cones and began backing out of the store, eyes wide with appreciation for Ethel's, and even Livy's, bullying.

Ethel inched closer to the obviously uncomfortable clerk. "Just what do you get out of gossiping about other people anyway, Alberta? Is your own life so utterly boring that you have to make stuff up about others just to pass the time? Or is it that your own life is so pathetic that you need to make others feel pathetic?" Ethel ridiculed, still making her way toward Alberta.

"I don't know what you are talking about, Ethel," Alberta tried to sound forceful, but the fact that she was continuing to back away, divulged her worry.

Livy was marinating in the beauty of the moment and let out a "Ha!" Alberta's head snapped to glare at the teenager.

Alberta pointed to Livy. "Why in the world would you listen to that little brat? She's nothing but a spoiled, rotten batch of trouble."

Ethel stopped and put her hands on her hips and scowled. "I'll take her spoiled, rotten character over your holier-than-thou one any day, Alberta!" she pointed at the much smaller woman. "At least she's not so low that she has to resort to lying about people just to get attention!"

By that time, Mary Ann and the other ladies had made their way to the front of the store and were surrounding the soda tables, mouths agape.

"Poo!" Alberta said waving her hand, trying to shoo off Ethel like she did to Livy. Shooing Ethel, however, was the wrong action to take and Ethel lunged at her.

"If you ever wave your prissy, little, manicured hands at me again, Alberta, I will break them off," Ethel challenged through clenched teeth. "I'm not some kid you can push around and brush off like I'm a nobody. Put them out here again. I dare you." She lurched at Alberta again.

Alberta jumped back before directing her attention to Mary Ann. "Are you going to let her talk to me that way?" she asked.

Mary Ann had way too much common sense to get in the middle of the catfight before her. "You heard her Alberta," Mary Ann answered. "She's ready to rip your hands off. I'm not about to mess with her."

"Well, I'll be," Alberta puffed, straightening herself up. "I don't believe this! You are going to let your employee act this way in the middle of the store? This is nothing short of harassment!"

Mary Ann, who had often found herself on the wrong end of Alberta's condemnation, decided to join ranks with Livy and Ethel. "Alberta, I think you can only handle one fight today. If I were you, I wouldn't pick another one," she threatened.

"Poo!" Alberta said again with new found courage. "This is absolutely ridiculous!" she made her way from behind the counter ranting all the way. "You all have just lost your minds and I don't have to put up with this! I'm going home where I am appreciated!" She huffed before she dramatically stormed out the door.

The women watched as Alberta scurried toward her car, which was parked in front of the vacant building next door. Livy turned to Ethel who was still seething while Mary Ann and the others looked at each other trying to figure out what had just happened.

"Ethel," Livy began, but no more got the words out before the door sprung open and Alberta reappeared.

Every eye turned to watch with interest as to what was about to unfold. Alberta huffed at Livy before brushing her aside with a whisk of her hand. She then went behind the soda fountain to retrieve her coat and purse.

Livy, not being able to help herself, started laughing before Alberta admonished her.

Alberta spit as she shooed the girl out of her way again. "You little urchin."

"You better watch it, Alberta," Ethel warned her.

Alberta raised her hand to "poo" Ethel, but remembered her threat and thought better of it.

When Alberta had exited her final time, Livy couldn't resist. "Only Alberta could go and ruin her own exit!" she cackled. Ethel turned and scowled at the girl, letting it be known she didn't think Livy was funny.

Seeing Ethel was still in a foul mood, Mary Ann and the others retreated back to their stations leaving just Ethel and Livy left to stare at one another.

Ethel took a deep breath trying to calm herself down before she spoke.

"Livy, you should not have started a fight in the middle of the store. This is a business and not a place for your amusement," she lectured. "In the future, I suggest you conduct private business in private," Ethel pursed her lips, shaming the girl.

Livy wanted to protest. After all, she hadn't been the one to start the fight. But, then she realized Ethel wasn't really mad at her and just needed a place to release her frustration.

"Yes ma'am," she said, obediently. "I won't do it again."

Chapter Seventeen

A Change of Plans

*E*thel tried to calm down by busying herself refilling the candy counter. Livy perched on a soda canister reliving the past few minutes. The phone rang. Still, in a state, she answered quite brusquely.

"Who peed in your Post Toasties?" Stevy asked.

"Alberta," Livy growled.

"What did she do now?"

"Same ole crap; just causing trouble. Anyway, what's up?"

"Well, I just got off the phone with Brandon, and we won't be going to Maiden tonight."

"Oh man," Livy whined, "Why not?"

"It's the Toilet Bowl," Stevy excitedly announced.

"Holy Cow, I totally forgot about that." Livy couldn't believe she had let such a big event slip her mind.

The Toilet Bowl was the annual football scrimmage between the varsity and junior varsity football teams. It started out being called the Orange and Black Game, since the school's mascot was the Tiger. But about ten years earlier, when neither team could get the ball five yards down the field because of all the fumbling and bad plays, it was appropriately renamed.

The referees were overheard comparing the game to a particularly bad bowl game for the Oklahoma Sooners.

"This is a total catastrophe. It reminds me of last year's Orange Bowl," one said.

"Orange Bowl, hell," said the other. "This is more like a Toilet Bowl." And it stuck. It was now and always would be The Toilet Bowl.

"Okay," Livy acknowledged, while trying to regroup. "What's the plan now?"

"Well Brandon, Jakey, and Mitch will all be playing, so let's go to the game. Then, we can walk them off the field," Stevy replied.

Walking the football players off the field was a Friday night tradition. If a girl's boyfriend played, she would escort him from the field following the game. For girls who didn't have a boyfriend, asking a player to escort them was a way for a girl to let them know she was interested.

"That's a great idea, Stevy," Livy agreed, "except for the fact that I don't have a boyfriend to walk off the field."

"What if I have Brandon call Mitch and ask him if you can walk him off the field tonight?" Stevy offered to accelerate the process.

Livy gasped. "Don't you dare! I couldn't stand it if he rejected me in front of everybody. I would completely die!" She revved up the dramatics again. "If he says no, come Monday all those stupid high school cheerleaders will be making fun of me. I will never be able to hold my head up again. My life will be ruined!"

"Wait a minute!" Stevy tried to get her friend's attention and stop the tirade. "Nobody is going to know but you, me, and Brandon. Come on, Livy. If you really want to go out with him, now's the time to make your move. Just let me call Brandon."

"Don't you dare," Livy half-heartedly responded, knowing it was probably her best chance to snag the object of her affections. She paused a few more moments trying to make the jump, although not quite being able to do it. "Let me just think about it some more and then I'll call you back."

"Okay, your loss," her best friend tried goading her one more time. "Spend the rest of your life as a wall flower, never dating, never having fun with the rest of us. You can just be alone forever and..."

"I get the picture, Stevy," Livy interupted. "I'm well aware that this may be the only chance I have to not be a spinster for the rest of my life."

Livy wholeheartedly subscribed to the histrionics, at the same time Ethel, who had been eavesdropping, rolled her eyes.

Chapter Eighteen

The Mystery Deepens

The phone rang again, and Ethel answered it. "Hold on a minute, I'll get her," she said into the receiver. "Livy, it's for you. Don't stay on long, our customers need to be able to get through." Ethel handed Livy the phone along with a slight scowl.

"Hello," Livy said in sultry Elizabeth Taylor like voice.

"Hello," a prissy, sultry voice mimicked back.

"What do you want now, Michael?" Livy moaned, annoyed that he was mocking her.

"How quickly they forget," Michael tisked. "You told me to call you back after I talked to Richy."

"Oh yeah, I forgot. Did he have a girl with him?"

"Nope, he said there weren't any girls there."

"That makes no sense," Livy shook her head. "Surely my granny didn't mistake a guy for a girl."

"I don't know," Michael answered. "He just said he was alone."

"Hmm," Livy thought a moment, "I don't know, maybe Granny is getting senile or old timer's disease," she theorized aloud.

"It's Alzheimer's, Livy."

"Who is?" she asked.

"The disease," Michael answered.

"What disease?" the less than brilliant young woman replied.

"Never mind," Michael gave up."

Hey, are you going to the Toilet Bowl tonight?" she quickly changed the subject.

"Honneee," he crooned, "you know I love watching those players, I uh mean football," he caught himself.

"Oh my gosh, Michael. You are so weird."

"Back at you girlfriend," he chirped. "What time are you going?"

"I guess about 6:30 since it starts at 7:00. Why?"

"Are you going to drive? Cause if you do, I want you to swing by and pick me up on your way," he responded.

Lester was usually oblivious, so most of the kids Livy's age had been driving since their early teens. Livy was no exception.

"Michael, you live across the street from the football field," Livy exasperatingly sighed.

"I know that," he retorted as if the girl was dumb. "But I can't have people see me walking. What will they think?"

"Ummm, that you are walking?" she responded.

"No, no, no, Livy. You just don't get what it takes to have the cool factor, do you?"

Livy humphed at Michael's dig. "Well, I can't pick you up anyway. My dad won't let me take his truck ever since I ran into the convenience store and then backed into that old lady that was double-parked behind me.

The phone went silent for a moment. "You did what?" Michael finally managed. "You hit the convenience store and someone parked behind you?"

"Yeah, but it wasn't my fault. I don't know why my dad is blaming me," she complained.

"Okay, I'll bite, tell me how you managed to hit an entire store and a parked car."

"First," Livy began to explain, "I hit the clutch instead of the brake."

"Okay, I can see that, but how do you back into a car that you know is double-parked behind you?" he snickered.

"I forgot she was there."

"Nuh uh." Michael acted as if he didn't believe her. "How in the heck did you forget she was there?!"

"Cause I had to check the mirror and make sure my makeup still looked good," Livy exhaled as if he should have known that.

Michael laughed out loud. "Oh my God, well, that settles it. I don't want to ride with you now anyway. It's no wonder your dad won't let you drive, Livy."

"I'm telling you it wasn't my fault," she protested. "It doesn't matter though. I'm not sure when or if he'll let me drive again." She sulked. "He said I was the worst woman driver he had ever seen and that included my Granny Belle."

"Darn," Michael replied. "I guess I'll just have to walk, but I don't know what my fans will think."

"I hate to break this to you Michael," Livy smirked, "but the only fans you have are dead people."

"Reerrr," he responded, mimicking a hissing cat.

"I've got to go," Livy tried to abruptly end the call. "Ethel is giving me the evil eye," she whispered, "and today is not a day I want to mess with her."

"Okay, I'll see you tonight," Michael said, making kissy noises into the phone.

Livy rolled her eyes. "You are so weird."

"And so proud of it," he haughtily remarked.

Chapter Nineteen

Tooter

*A*fter her phone call, Livy sorted through the nearby candy carousel, finally settling on a Zero bar. She picked up the Archie Comic Book she had been reading earlier and settled down on a soda canister.

Honk. Honk. Livy recognized the horn, which sounded like a goose in heat. It was Tooter's, one of the town's more interesting, but loveable residents.

Tooter had grown up in Konawa and could be seen all over town almost every day on his big 1940's red and white Schwinn bicycle. It was said that he had once been an exceptionally smart boy until he was hit in the head by a flying board in the tornado of 1961. The injury kept the then ten-year-old in a coma for two months before he woke up. When he did, he was to forever remain the young child he had been when he was hit.

Tooter made deliveries for Ralph's, Steelman's, and on Thursdays for the weekly newspaper. Everywhere he went, he would announce his arrival by honking the horn on his old bike. It was as familiar a sound at the drugstore as the phone ringing because Tooter loved comic books. Once a week, he brought in all his spending money to buy whatever the store had.

"Hi, ya'!" Tooter grinned to Livy as he walked through the front door waving a lanky, bony arm at the girl.

Tooter was in his mid-twenties. He was as lean as a stick and had legs that were abnormally long, especially for his bike. It was not uncommon to see him peddling down the street, knees thumping the handlebars as he rode. He had dark brown hair that he still kept in a 1950's style buzz cut and big black framed glasses that made his eyes look two sizes too big for his face. The glasses sat atop a sharp Romanesque arched nose and above two very thin lips which Tooter licked all the time, making them unusually red.

"Hi Tooter," Livy greeted him in return. "I've got the new Archie comic book if you want it," she said, holding it up for him to see.

"Nah, I already got that one last week," he answered. "I want Superman and Richie Rich." He pointed to the magazine rack where they were housed.

"Are you through with your errands today?" Livy queried the ten-year-old adult.

"Nah, Ralph doesn't have Mrs. Moody's order ready yet, so I thought I would get a Vanilla Coke and some comic books while I'm waiting."

"One Vanilla Coke coming up," Livy said. "What size?"

"I want that really big one," he said pointing to the largest cup behind the counter. "I'm real thirsty today. I had to ride out past the school to the Rainbow's. I'm hot."

"How 'bout some extra vanilla then," Livy smiled at him.

"Yeah," Tooter gleamed, "I want extra vanilla. It's my favorite."

Livy fixed the cola and gave it to Tooter. He began sucking on the straw for all he was worth.

"Ahhh, that's good," he said, finally taking a breath before heading for the comic book rack.

"You need anything else, Tooter?" Livy asked before she returned to her seat.

"Nah, I'm just going to look at these," he said fingering the comics and licking his lips. He buried his large nose in the rack searching for just the perfect ones.

"Tooter?" Livy hesitantly interrupted.

"Um," he replied, too engrossed in his search to really pay any attention.

"Do you remember the tornado that blew the town away?" she asked him anyway.

"Nope, but my mama told me all about it," he said, turning away from the rack and gaining interest in the topic.

"My grandpa told me some stories about it too," Livy said. "But not much really. I wasn't born yet so I don't know anything other than what he's said."

"My mama said that this used to be a really big place," he said, pointing outside. "She said they had hotels and a train depot and lots and lots of stores of all kinds." He was getting excited. "I was hit by a board, and it made me forget. But my mama likes to tell me about everything that used to be here."

"Yeah, my grandpa told me they even had four drugstores here at one time," Livy marveled. "The only one that stayed though was this one and one other that closed later. I wonder why though?" Livy pondered aloud.

"Mama said it was because everybody was pretty poor, and no one had the money to start over," Tooter answered her question. "She said that afternoon when it hit, nobody was expectin' it. She said that's why I got hit on the head. She said that if she would have known it was comin' that she would have already had me in the cellar."

"Yeah, my grandpa said it was a good thing that he was out of town. He took my older siblings to the circus in Maiden. He said when they got home, the bed that my middle sister and older brother would have been in was completely smashed by a tree that came through their house. He said if they would have been in that bed napping, they would be dead." Livy dramatically popped her eyes out.

He shook his head. "Yeah," Tooter agreed, "My mama said it was a miracle that I wasn't dead. She said I slept for two months and she didn't think I was gonna' wake up, but I did." He nodded again. "I just don't remember anything from before then though." Tooter looked back at the comic books for a moment.

Eventually, he rejoined the conversation "I kind of wish I remembered. I think it would be neat to be in a tornado. I've tried really hard to remember it, but I just can't."

Livy nodded with sympathy.

Tooter turned back around to look at Livy. "I sometimes make things up about it and tell my mama. She says that's not how it happened though. Once I told her that I thought I was riding my bicycle really fast and I knew there was a big board coming after me and I rode faster and faster!" He was excited with the story he was telling. "I was getting away from it, but it kept gaining on me. I finally got to my house. I got off my bike and ran to the front door. Just as I was opening the door, SMASH!" he yelled waving his arms like he was falling. "It hit me right smack in the head."

"Is that what happened?" Livy asked, excited too because she had never heard the real story.

"Nah," he said looking sad. "Mama said I was helping her take the laundry off the clothes line before it got all wet and all the sudden a loose board from my dog's house whipped off and hit me on my head. She said I passed out plum cold."

"It's still a good story," Livy said, trying to make Tooter feel better.

"Nah," he sulked. "Not as good as me tryin' to outrun it."

"Did you find the Richie Rich?" Livy asked, changing the subject.

"Nah, not yet. But I will," he said as he turned back to the rack.

Ethel came up the aisle from the back of the store.

"Hello Tooter," she said, waving to the child in adult's clothing.

"Hi, Ms. Ethel," he murmured shyly.

Tooter was at home with kids his own age, or at least the ones he thought were his own age, but he was bashful around adults. It was for that reason he honked his horn on deliveries. The horn would announce his arrival and allowed him to avoid saying anything to his adult customers.

"Are you busy today?" Ethel asked him.

"Yes em'," he replied, although it was barely audible.

"Well, good. Keeping busy is a good way to be. It keeps you out of trouble," Ethel philosophized.

"Yes, em'," he replied again.

Tooter didn't want to spend any more time on the conversation than was necessary, so he grabbed the two comics he wanted and laid fifty cents on the counter for the comic books, and another thirty for the soda, before hurrying out of the store.

"Bye Tooter," Livy said after him.

"Bye," he said, trying to avoid Ethel's gaze.

"Bye, Tooter," Ethel said, determined to get in some more conversation.

"Yes em'," he said, ducking out.

Chapter Twenty

Men in Black

As soon as Tooter left, Ethel told Livy to sweep the outdoor rug at the entrance to the building. Livy started to get the broom from behind the fountain, but before she could, two looming and lanky figures entered the store. She had never seen the tall men before. They wore black felt cowboy hats, cowboy boots, and jeans that were starched so heavily that they looked like they would crack if they bent over.

The taller man had jet-black curly hair and a trimmed, black goatee. His boots were black ostrich skin, the kind with pointy toes. He walked toward Livy with strides that were as long as a giraffe's.

"Can I help you?" Livy asked.

"Just coffee, ma'am," he said, tipping his hat.

"Make that two," added his partner. "Black."

The two men pulled seats out from one of the tables and tried to place their unnaturally long legs underneath. Neither could manage without their knees bumping the table causing the glass sugar dispenser to wobble. Finally, both gave up, opting to lean back in the metal soda chairs and stretch their long legs.

Livy eyed each of them as she poured the hot coffee into mugs. The second man was a little heavier than the first with limp, brown hair and big gold-rimmed glasses. The back pocket of his Wrangler's revealed a white circle, where his Skoal can had worn into his jeans.

Livy put the mugs in front of them. "Here you go," she said, still looking them over.

"Thank you, Miss," the one with the glasses said.

"Can I get you anything else?" Livy asked, still wondering who they were.

"Nope, that should do it," the taller one replied.

She left them and went back behind the counter, trying to stay close enough to eavesdrop and see if she could pick up any clues as to their identity. It wasn't common to have strangers in town. When there were, they usually didn't turn out to be strangers at all, but someone's relative instead.

"Well, this is an interesting place," the guy in glasses said to the curly headed one.

"Yeah, it is at that," he replied.

"Man, have you ever seen a fatter policeman in your life than that Lester guy?" Glasses laughed while circling his arms around a fake big stomach.

"Boy, he is a big one ain't he? Curly responded.

"I wonder how long it will take us to get this thing solved so we can get out of BFE," Glasses remarked.

Livy wondered to herself what or where was BFE.

Curly smirked. "Shouldn't take too long. This place probably only has two residents. It's got to be one of em'."

Glasses cackled. "Yeah, I ain't sure I've ever been to any place much smaller than this."

Livy picked up the coffee pot and returned to the table to refill their cups.

"Still doing okay?" she asked.

"Doing just fine, Miss," Curly said. "You live here?" he asked as if she would work there if she lived in some cooler place.

"Yeah, most of my life," she said, lifting the coffee pot between them.

"What in the world do you all do here for fun?" he asked.

"Nothing; this place is really boring," she rolled her eyes, trying to let them know her sophistication far outweighed the two-bit town.

"You work here all the time?" Glasses said, turning his head to face her.

"Just after school sometimes, and on Saturday's. My mom owns it," she replied, trying to impress them.

"Yeah?" Curly acknowledged.

"Yeah, she's a pharmacist. Are you two from around here?" Livy surprised herself that she had mustered enough courage to just come right out and ask.

"Naw. We're from Oklahoma City. We're with the OSBI and we had to do a little work down here." Glasses said.

"Oh, yeah," Livy replied. "I heard you guys were going to help Lester with those women who are robbing our old people." Livy started getting excited realizing the two men were big time police investigators.

"You know about the robberies?" Curly asked. He raised an eyebrow.

"Everybody knows about them," Livy answered. "Everybody knows everything that goes on around here. It's one of the reasons I hate this place so much," she said, fabricating disgust.

"You know about the ones in Paxton too?" Glasses asked.

Paxton was another little town about ten miles north of Konawa, but it was even smaller and had no policeman at all.

"No," Livy was surprised. "You mean people in Paxton are being robbed too?" Her eyes got wide realizing Konawa was obviously part of a crime spree of mass proportions.

"Yep, they had three up there," Curly said. "So, what do you know about these robberies?"

"Just that my granny was almost robbed," Livy relayed. "Luckily, she knew not to let them in her house to use the phone because I warned her about it," Livy said, with much self-importance.

"What do you mean she knew not to let them in?" Glasses inquired.

"Well, she had read about some of the robberies in the paper and that the women would ask to use people's phones and then tie them up and rob them. But she was still leaving her door unlocked." Livy acted as if she were perturbed with her grandmother. "I kept getting on to her about leaving her door unlocked, but she's stubborn and thinks she knows best." Livy shook her head and tisked. "I swear, sometimes, you just can't tell these old people anything," she blustered, still full of her self-importance.

"Did your grandma get a good look at the people?" Curly asked.

"She said she did, but she didn't recognize them. She's lived around here for a long, long time, so I would think if they were from here, she would have known it," Livy informed, thrilled to be offering her wisdom and insight to the investigation. She decided it was probably the most important thing she had ever done.

"Does your grandma get out much? I mean does she keep up with any new people that move into town?" Curly asked.

"Well, no," Livy answered, unsure of the question.

"So, if somebody was new in town, she probably wouldn't know them then," Glasses stated.

"Umm, no, I guess not." Livy paused. "You think somebody that's moved here recently is doing this?" she asked, hoping they would reveal their speculations.

"No. Not saying that at all," Glasses responded. "How long has your grandma been staying at home?"

"What do you mean?"

"I mean how many years has she been not getting out much?"

"Oh, gosh," Livy pulled out one of the chairs at the table and sat down. "It's been at least five or six years because once

I got old enough to get her groceries and stuff for her, my dad and I've been doing it." She sat the coffee pot in front of her. "Before that, she would walk into town every week and get them herself. She doesn't even know how to drive."

Glasses looked at her. "Well, she probably doesn't know the people who've been here for at least that long."

"Oh yeah," Livy offered, becoming disappointed in her detective skills.

"Do you think your grandma would know the people if she saw them again? Curly asked.

"Maybe," Livy shrugged, becoming excited again. "Why? Do you have pictures of the people that did it?"

"No, we don't know who did it. But when we get a suspect, we might want your grandmother to identify them," Curly explained.

"She might get scared if she had to talk to you. She's just a little old widow that lives alone. She's pretty shy and she doesn't like anybody making a fuss over her." Livy wasn't really keen on the idea of the two accosting her grandmother.

Curly sensed her hesitation and tried to squelch it. "Well, we probably won't need to, but just in case."

"Oh my gosh!" Livy abruptly sat up, remembering the Mrs. Spivey incident. "I just talked to my granny a little while ago because her neighbor died and I wanted to make sure she was okay..." she prattled without taking a breath. "She told me that she thought she had seen one of the ladies that tried to rob her at Mrs. Spivey's house. But I called Michael, and he told me that there was no..."

"Slow down, slow down," Curly interrupted her by putting up his hand. "Who's Mrs. Spivey? And who's Michael?"

"Mrs. Spivey is the neighbor that died, and Michael is my friend that works at the funeral home," Livy answered. "When Granny told me that she thought she saw that woman, I called Michael to find out who she was. I wanted to know if Richy had a girlfriend with him and...."

"Wait a minute," Glasses held up his own hand, getting irritated. "Who's Richy and what does he have to do with this and...," Glasses trailed off and looked at Curly. "What the hell is she talking about?"

"Good question." Curly confirmed his partner's confusion and then looked at Livy. "Let's try this a little differently, okay?" he asked her.

"Um, yeah," Livy replied, perplexed at the problem.

"Okay good. Let us ask you some questions and you just answer real short. If we need more information, we'll have you fill us in some more, okay?"

"Okay," she shrugged, a little bothered that the two had interrupted her incredibly interesting story.

"Okay, Miss, I'm Agent Douglas," Curly said. "And this is Agent Brett." he gestured to his partner with the glasses. "What's your name?"

"I'm Livy Stephens," Livy answered, awkwardly sticking out her hand to shake theirs, although she wasn't sure whose to shake first. A spastic flapping ensued until Curly grabbed her hand put it down on the table.

"Hi, Livy. Okay, your grandmother thought she was about to be robbed, is that right?" Curly asked.

"Right," she said, wondering if he thought she was slow in the head or something.

"And she saw the perpetrators, right?"

Livy looked at him with a blank stare. "You think they were sweaty? My granny never said anything about that." Livy shook her head. "She just said it was an older woman and a younger one and that one was fat and had stringy, greasy hair," the bewildered girl offered.

Curly laughed. "No, not perspirators, perpetrators. It means the people that committed the crime."

Glasses had been putting some Skoal in his mouth and snorted so hard it went up his nose. He spewed little bits of the dried leafs onto the table. He coughed in a choking fit until Curly hit him on the back. He looked up with tears in his eyes. Livy turned red, embarrassed that she had not known what they meant.

"Sorry," Glasses still choking, tried to regain his composure. "Just got a little too much Skoal in my mouth." He tried to hide his amusement to avoid further embarrassing the teen. Livy knew what he was attempting to do and wanted to sink under the table and pretend that the big city slickers didn't know what a hick she really was.

"Okay, Livy," Curly jumped back in, in order to stabilize the situation. "Your grandma got a good look at the women who she thought were going to rob her, and she said she didn't recognize them. Is that right?" He was now taking notes with a small pad and pencil he had pulled from his shirt pocket.

"Yeah, that's right," Livy answered. "My grandma knew not to…"

"Okay, remember, you just keep your answers short, and we'll ask you to elaborate if we need you to," he reminded her.

"Okay," she replied, sulking and thinking that she had a lot of good information that she could tell them if they would just let her.

"What is your Grandma's name?" Glasses asked.

"Maudie Stephens," Livy answered.

"Where does Mrs. Stephens live?" Curly asked.

"By the park," she said, pointing to the north.

"What's her address?" he tried again.

Livy had no idea because she never mailed her grandmother anything, but she didn't want the men to think that not only was she a hick, but a stupid hick.

"What street does she live on?" Curly asked as if he thought she didn't know what the word address meant.

Livy blushed, embarrassed that she had dug this hole for herself. "Oh, what is the name of that street?" she asked herself as if she had just forgotten. "Darn, I can't remember it for the life of me. I don't ever mail her anything. Anyway, she lives three houses up from the park on the opposite side of the street from the armory."

"Okay," Curly sighed, obviously getting irritated. "How do we get to the park from here?'

"That's easy," Livy was regaining her confidence, "just go to the end of Main, make a right and turn left at the gas station. That's the street my granny lives on. It runs right into the park."

"Okay, good. We may want to visit your grandmother, but we'll decide that later," he informed her.

Livy interrupted. "If you do, you need to take me with you because she won't open her door to anyone anymore after what happened. But she'll let you in if I'm with you, and besides, it will keep her from being scared," the protective girl explained.

"Okay, we'll do that," Curly agreed. "Now, you said something about a Richy. Who's Richy?"

"He's the other guy that works at the funeral home with my friend, Michael," Livy answered.

"And what did you say about his girlfriend?" Curly asked.

"He doesn't have a girlfriend," Livy replied.

Glasses looked at her, cocking his head. "I thought you said he had a girlfriend," he furrowed his brow.

"No, I said he didn't have a girlfriend," Livy corrected.

Glasses shook his head in disagreement. "You said something about a girl being with him by your grandma's house," he countered.

"No, I didn't," Livy took on an argumentative tone.

"Yes, you said you asked Mike about…"

"Michael," Livy interrupted, "He never goes by Mike. He hates that name. He says it's too redneckish. He says it makes him sound like a ball buster," she explained, having no idea what a ball buster was.

"Oh, really," Glasses said, raising the glasses from his face. "Well my name is Mike and I'm not a redneck," he pointed out sarcastically.

"Hey, I'm not the one who said it. Michael is," Livy retorted.

"Hold on," Curly jumped in, "Let's get back on subject."

Mike the non-redneck agent, sulked but leaned back in his chair waiting on Curly to continue.

"Tell us again what you said about Richy, please Miss Stephens."

Livy liked being called Miss Stephens thinking it showed a great respect for her and her information.

"I said that when my granny told me she thought she saw the woman who tried to rob her at Mrs. Spivey's..."

Curly interrupted again. "Mrs. Spivey is who?"

"She's my granny's neighbor that died last night."

"Okay, go on," he instructed.

"I said that when she thought she saw her, I called Michael to see if he had picked up Mrs. Spivey, but he said Richy did. So, I asked him if Richy had taken a girlfriend with him."

"Why?" Glasses asked.

"Why what?" Livy was becoming more confused by the moment.

"Why did you ask if he had taken his girlfriend?"

"He doesn't have a girlfriend," she reiterated, clearly tired of the banter.

"But you just said…"

Curly cut in. "So, he didn't take a girlfriend with him to pick up Mrs. Spivey?"

Glasses looked at Curly like he must be a genius for being able to follow Livy's story.

"That's right. Michael said Richy didn't have a girlfriend. So, I asked Michael what girl was there when they picked up Mrs. Spivey."

"And?" Curly asked.

"He asked Richy, and Richy said there was no girl, just him and the police."

"So, your grandmother was wrong about there being a girl there?"

"I guess, maybe," Livy acknowledged. "But Michael thought that it might have been one of Mrs. Spivey's kids or something."

"Was it?" Curly asked, still writing in his notebook.

"No, I'm pretty sure she only had sons. But still, maybe it was a daughter-in-law or something. My granny is still sharp as a tack, and she sees pretty well. She hasn't worn glasses since she got her cataracts removed. But I guess since it was dark, maybe she saw a man that looked like a woman or something? You never can tell, she maybe…."

Glasses interrupted this time. "Well, we will check into it and see if there were any daughter-in-laws there. How old is your grandma anyway?"

"Seventy-four. But like I said, she's still sharp as a tack," Livy defended her grandmother's sensibilities.

"I'm sure she is," Curly conceded. "We will contact you if we need to go see her," he said, pushing his chair back to stand. Glasses followed.

"Here is my card. If you hear anything else, you can give me a call, okay?" he informed her while extending the small white card with a little blue seal of the state of Oklahoma and the letters OSBI below.

"Sure," Livy excitedly took the card, happy to be a part of helping solve the town's epic crime spree.

"Okay, Miss Stephens, you have a good day now, ya' hear?" Curly nodded, tipping his hat.

"You too," Livy answered as she watched them leave.

Chapter Twenty-One

BFE

"What's BFE?" Livy asked Michael as soon as he answered the funeral home phone.

"Well hello to you too!" he singsonged.

"Michael, what's BFE?" she asked again, becoming irritated that he wouldn't answer her question.

"It's this God-forsaken hell hole where we reside," he answered. "Why?"

Livy tried to figure out how God-forsaken hell hole belonged to the letters BFE. "I don't get it."

"What don't you get, honey?" Michael admonished. "I mean, it's so obvious, isn't it?"

"Ugh…no," Livy replied. "I still don't get it. Just tell me you little twerp."

"Oooh, testy, testy. Is Auntie Flo visiting today, Dahling?"

"No! Don't ask me things like that!" Livy hissed. "Just tell me what BFE means!"

"First, you tell me why, Miss Priss," Michael insisted.

"Okay, there were these two guys that just came in here. And – oh my gosh, you are not going to believe it! They are from the OSB and they just asked me a bunch of questions about the robberies, and I overheard…"

"Wait a minute, sister," Michael lisped. "Don't you mean the OSBI?"

"Yeah, that's what I said," Livy was aggravated that Michael interrupted. "Anyway…"

"Well, I just want to go on record," he butted in again, "that you said OSB, not OSBI."

"So, what?!" Livy cried. "Who cares? What the heck is OSBI anyway?"

"Oklahoma State Bureau of Investigation," Michael smugly relayed. "We have to talk to them sometimes on unattended deaths."

"Who cares?!" Livy cried again. "Shut up and let me tell you this!"

"Okay, Queen of Drama," Michael snipped. "Go ahead."

"Okay, I was kind of eaves dropping when these two OBI agents came in…"

Michael sighed in disgust. "Oklahoma Blood Institute," he murmured.

"What?" Livy asked.

"Nothing," he sighed again. "Finish your story."

"And one of them, Agent – oh crap, I can't remember his name – said to the other that he wanted to get out of BFE, and I think he was talking about here, but it sounded like it was some sort of code word or something. I thought maybe they knew I was listening and didn't want to give away any secrets of their case or something and so they talked in code," Livy created.

Michael began laughing hysterically. "Oh, honey!" he squealed. "You are just a few blueberries short of a Pop Tart, aren't you?"

"What the heck does that mean?" Livy got defensive.

"I cannot believe that little brain of yours makes A's. How many of the teachers are you bribing or worse, sleeping with?" he crowed.

"Hey that is not funny," Livy warned. "All of my teachers are women, and I don't have a thing for people of my own gender, unlike somebody I know," she needled.

Michael ignored her innuendo. "Well, it's a good thing," he snorted, "because you would have to be some kind of woman to get them to pass your dumb ass!" He giggled, completely cracking himself up at Livy's expense.

"Look, just because I don't speak some top-secret agent code doesn't mean I'm dumb," she said with a pout. "I can't help it if I don't get out of this stupid little Podunk town enough to know this stuff."

"Exactly!" Michael shouted. "That's exactly right!"

"What is? What are you talking about?"

"BFE is short for Bumfuck, Egypt," Michael clarified.

"What's that code for?" Livy asked still not understanding.

"No, you goofy broad. Bumfuck, Egypt is a way of saying little; not on the map; insignificant; desert; non-existent; in the middle of nowhere. They were saying they wanted to leave this, as you so eloquently put it, Podunk town." Michael exhaled, exasperated.

"Oh, I get it – I think," Livy stopped to make sure she really was grasping the concept. "Why Egypt though?"

"Because it is desert, everywhere you look you see nothing but nothingness. Believe me, the last place you want to ever be stranded in the middle of, is an Egyptian Desert. I mean, honey, there is just sand everywhere, and it gets into every little crack and crevice you've got." Michael started a tirade of his own. "Oh and, my gosh, there are like, no toilets. You just have to go squat out behind a dune or something. And let me tell you, girl, there are creatures in the desert that you don't want anywhere near the areas of your body that are squatting."

"Um…okay."

Michael had relayed way more about BFE than Livy wanted to know, but she was delighted to find out that all along, her feelings about her hometown were correct. "So, what I have suspected about this two-bit town really is true," she boasted. "And I now have two highly intelligent Oklahoma City agents backing me up," she congratulated herself.

"Yeah," Michael agreed. "Margaret tells me all the time that I am being foolish when I say I wanna get out of here. She says leaving this town is not going to solve any of my problems," he relayed. "Little does she know. There's just not a lot of picking in this place," Michael thought aloud.

"Who's Margaret?" Livy asked.

"You know, Mr. Winter, the owner's wife."

"Why did she say leaving won't solve your problems? What problems have you got? Livy pried.

"She knows I'm gay, Livy."

"She knows your gay?" Livy could not believe that Michael had just confessed his greatest secret to her, and she tried to think fast on her feet so he wouldn't feel uncomfortable that he had revealed his long-hidden identity.

"Well, how did she find out you were gay?" Livy acted completely unsurprised and nonchalant, although she was worried that someone that old – like thirty-something – would totally flip out.

"I think she figured it out when she caught me trying on the lipstick the family brought in for Mrs. Pomeroy," Michael sighed.

"Yep, that would do it alright," Livy laughed. "Was she okay with it though?" she broached.

"I guess. The very next day, she brought me a lipstick of hers and said it was a better color for me."

Livy thought that was cool and exceedingly progressive of the woman.

"Anyway," Michael cut into her thoughts. "there's nothing for me here after high school," he admitted. "There's only one other gay guy in town, and he's my cousin. Plus, he's about as opposite of tall, dark, and handsome as you can get," Michael grumbled.

Livy had no idea how to give gay dating advice so she changed the subject.

"Well, thanks for clearing up the BFE stuff for me. Dang," she griped, "I wish it would have been some really cool secret agent code though. Nothing good ever happens around here," she pouted.

"You speak the truth, sister," Michael said. "Oh well, see you at the Toilet Bowl."

"See ya," she said hanging up the phone.

Chapter Twenty-Two

Monkey Shit

*L*ivy hung up the phone and walked to the back of the store. She opened the door to the storage area, which also housed the gift-wrap area, Lucy the bookkeeper's office, and two-steps higher, the restroom.

She knocked on Lucy's door. Lucy was a sweet, little gray-haired lady with silver rimmed glasses and powder-soft peachy cheeks. Livy loved her, and unlike Alberta, she always seemed happy to see the girl.

"Hi, Lucy," Livy said, opening the office door.

"Well, hi dear," she said with a smile. "What are you up to today?"

"Nothing much," Livy sat down and started playing with the keys of a small manual typewriter that sat beside her. Across the front of the type-writer was taped a piece of paper that read:

1 2 3 4 5 6 7 8 9 0

M O N K E Y S H I T

"Lucy, why do you have the numbers one through zero and letters that spell out Monkey Shit on your typewriter?" Livy asked.

"Oh, that's just our pricing code," she answered.

"I don't understand," Livy looked bewildered.

"Well, you know the price labels we put on everything?" she asked.

"Yeah."

"Well, have you ever noticed that above the price there are letters?"

"Um…yeah, I guess," she said trying to actually remember.

"Well, those letters tell us how much we paid for something and what our markup is."

"What?" Livy remained confused.

"Okay, Sweetie, say we sell a bottle of aspirin for two-dollars, but our price was only one dollar. The price label would show $2.00, and above it would be the letters MTT. M for 1 and the T's for 0's. That tells your mom what her cost is, so if she needs to negotiate a price with someone, she can do it, and we can keep track of our cost when we do inventory," she explained.

"Who came up with Monkey Shit?" Livy asked, hoping it wasn't Lucy but assuming it was her own mother.

"The former owner." Lucy surprised her.

"You mean we still use their code? What if they want to buy something here? They'll know how much it costs," Livy became worried that the store might go bankrupt.

"Oh, it's highly unlikely," Lucy responded. "He's dead."

"Well, that's good." Livy was relieved.

Livy started pecking at the keys typing Monkey Shit over and over and becoming ever more impressed by the man that came up with such a good code. Then, she decided she should make up her own code for fun. After all, how hard could it be?

1 2 3 4 5 6 7 8 9 0 she typed.

T U R K E Y B O O B she wrote.

"Look, Lucy, I've got my own code," Livy said proudly.

Lucy turned to look at the girl's paper. "That won't work," Lucy shook her head.

"Why not?" Livy asked, taken aback that Lucy was not as impressed with her code making skills as she was.

"Because you've repeated two letters, the B and the O."

"So, what does that matter?"

"It matters a lot," Lucy answered, "because how are you going to know if the B stands for a seven or a zero? Or the O's for an eight or a nine? You can't have any letter twice or you won't know what number it represents."

"Oh wow, I never thought of that. This is going to be harder than I thought." Livy was even more impressed with the dead monkey shit guy than before.

1 2 3 4 5 6 7 8 9 0

T O A D W A R T E D

"Nope, two A's and two D's."

M U S T A R D B U T

"Nope, two T's and two U's."

"Dang, this is tough," Livy said aloud.

Lucy kept working on the columns she was adding, paying little attention to the girl, until she yelled.

"D I M P L E B U N S!" "I got it!" Livy yelled pulling the paper from the machine to show Lucy.

"Good Heavens Livy, you scared the mothballs out of me," Lucy declared.

"Sorry," the girl apologized. "But look, I made my own code."

"Dimple Buns," Lucy read aloud. "Yep, you did it. Dimple Buns is ten letters with none repeating."

"Hey, you think we can start using Dimple Buns in case some of the dead guy's relatives come in here?" Livy reasoned.

"Only if you want to go change labels on thousands of pieces of inventory," she laughed.

"Um...no, I don't think I want to do that," Livy backed off. "Monkey Shit is just fine."

"I think so too," Lucy said. "Besides, we've been using it so long I have all of the letters and numbers memorized to where I don't even have to think about it anymore. I'm too old to be changing now."

"You're not old, Lucy," Livy humored her. "You're a lot younger than my grannies."

"Not much, sugar," the woman smiled. "Anyway, I'm one of those old biddies that doesn't like change. Keep everything the same for me, and I'll be happy."

"Not me. I can't wait for things to change."

"Like what?" Lucy asked, turning to look at the girl.

"Like getting my driver's license and getting a boyfriend and getting a different job in Maiden where it's exciting and then leaving this little pothole and going someplace fun and amazing," she droned on.

"Oh now, Sugar," Lucy disagreed, "everybody your age wants to leave – not just people who live here, but even the kids who live in Maiden, and believe it or not, kids who live in Oklahoma City."

"No way," Livy argued. "They've got tons of stuff to do and places to go and tons of boys to pick from and friends to pick from. There's no way they could be as bored as we are here."

"You'd be surprised," Lucy asserted. "And you will be even more surprised to know that someday, you will probably be glad you grew up here. You may even want to come back here to live," she announced.

Livy gasped, unbelieving that Lucy would even say such a thing.

"She should have just slapped my face and called me a whore," Livy thought to herself.

"Lucy, no offense," Livy protested, "but, there is no way in H-E double hockey sticks that I will ever want to come back here and live. This place is the pits with a capital P. I would rather live in BFE!"

Lucy laughed.

"Come about twenty or thirty years from now, when I'm long gone, you just remember what I said," the sweet lady ministered. "You just might find out that this old woman knew a thing or two."

Livy sighed while getting up. "Well, I guess we'll see. But don't count on it. My mind is made up," she forcefully stated. "I'd rather have dimple buns."

Chapter Twenty-Three

Butter Bean

As Livy closed the door to Lucy's office, she heard Ethel yelling at everyone to get up to the front.

Mary Ann, Barbara, Lucy, and Livy all came squashing together outside the pharmacy door.

"What's the matter, Ethel?" Mary Ann yelled up at her. "What's wrong?"

"Come here!" she said waving them on. "Mrs. Oliver just stepped in and said someone is trying to jump off the roof of Hibbs' Appliances and commit suicide," she yelled.

"What the…?" Livy's mother said, heading for the door. "Are you sure?"

"Just look," Ethel answered. "There's a huge crowd up there. Lester has a bullhorn."

The group stepped out onto the sidewalk and one by one hurriedly made their way up the street, leaving the store completely unmanned.

"Oh, my gosh!" Livy squealed with excitement. "This is too cool!"

Barbara looked at her as if she had lost her mind.

"Who is it?" Lucy asked.

"I can't tell," Ethel answered, stretching her neck like an ostrich.

The group could hear Lester on his bullhorn. It sounded like mooing.

When they arrived at the back of the crowd, they could better make out the conversation taking place.

"Now just a moment here, young man," Lester pleaded. "Let's talk about this. Don't go and do something rash."

"Can you see anything yet, Ethel?" Lucy asked standing on her toes, trying to see over the assembly.

"Not yet," Ethel replied. "Let's get closer," she instructed the group while pushing people aside.

Mary Ann, who was in her stocking feet because of bunion problems called out. "Ethel, slow down."

Ethel finally made a path to the front of the gathering, directly across from the appliance store.

"Oh, Heavens," Barbara said, clasping her hand to her mouth. "There *IS* someone on the roof."

"Who is it?" Mary Ann asked, also standing tiptoed behind Ethel and Livy.

"Oh, my gosh!" Livy gasped, turning to the group. "It's Butter Bean!"

Butter Bean had graduated from high school about five years earlier. He was a short, rotund guy with a burr haircut and pop-bottle glasses. He was super fair skinned, almost albino looking. He had been nicknamed Butter Bean, because of his plump, white, round body.

Kids, who didn't have anything better to do on Saturday nights, would go to the grocery store and buy cans of butter beans. They would sneak up to the house where he still lived with his mother and butter bean his porch and sometimes his car.

Livy had only done it once and had never attempted it again since the previous summer when she, Michael and Bebe had tried to butter bean his car.

"Be quiet," Livy shhhhhed Michael, who was cackling out loud just at the thought of what they were about to do. "He's going to hear us, you Moron!"

"Get down," Bebe whispered, as the three snuck along the front hedges on their way to his car, which sat about five feet from their hiding place.

"Tee, hee, hee," Michael continued.

"Shut up, Michael! You're being too loud," Livy warned.

Bebe crept out from behind the hedge, sneaking up to the back bumper of the old tan car. She waved at Michael and Livy to follow.

"Snort!" Michael's laughing sounded like a pig in heat.

"Shut up, you Duffus," Livy hissed.

He put his hand over his mouth, but she could still see the silhouette of his shoulders shaking in the moonlight.

Bebe crawled around the side of the car farthest from the house. She whispered back at Livy.

"Give me the can opener."

Michael guffawed again.

"Shut up, Michael!" Bebe whisper-yelled.

Livy handed her the can opener, and she plopped down on her rump to open the three cans they had purchased.

Michael was holding his stomach, but snorting all the same.

"Michael, I swear I will kick your sissy butt if you don't shut up," Livy said, shoving him to the ground.

Michael couldn't stop snorting.

Bebe opened the cans, handing one to each of them. She tiptoed around the front of the car to get a better shot at the windshield. Livy stayed at the passenger door, and Michael snorted his way back to the trunk.

Just as the trio started dumping the beans, they heard a click – but not just any click – it was the click of a shotgun being cocked.

Bebe squealed.

"I'll teach you butt holes to mess with me," came another sissy voice from the porch.

"Run!" Livy screamed.

"Alley!" Bebe screamed heading toward the alley.

Michael took a dive behind the car and kind of rolled toward Bebe and Livy's escape route.

KaBoom!

"Holy cow! He's shooting at us!" Livy yelled to Michael.

"No shit, Sherlock!" he yelled back.

Livy could see Bebe's head bobbing as she ran ahead of her down the alley and she could hear Michael's squeaky little huffs panting behind them.

KaBoom!

"Aghhhhhh!" Michael squealed like he had been hit.

"Oh my God, Michael!" Livy screamed. "Are you okay?"

"Run," he yelled in his high-pitched girl voice. "Run like the wind!"

Bebe was already down the alley and out of sight. Livy picked up speed and rounded the corner at the end of the block. Michael came screeching in right behind them, almost knocking Livy down, before falling to the ground and panting like a dog.

"Oh my God!" he screeched. "Can you believe Butter Bean just shot at us?"

"I thought we were goners," Livy gasped for air, trying to catch her breath.

"I will never, ever, ever, again, butter bean Butter Bean!" Bebe exclaimed.

"We better get out of here, he may still be after us," Michael warned.

"Michael, let's go to your house. We can lay low and play pool, just in case somebody called Lester because of the shooting," Livy said.

Michael lived less than a block from their escape destination so the group headed to his house. Sure enough, they saw Lester driving by with his spotlight trained on the side streets and alleys by Butter Bean's house, and they high-tailed it out of there, never getting caught.

As Livy looked up at the hefty little man, who was obviously an emotional wreck, she felt great remorse for what she had done to him. It hadn't occurred to her that what she had thought of as harmless Saturday night fun might not have been so harmless. She wondered if Butter Bean had wanted to die because of them and all the others. She got a sick feeling in her stomach.

"Okay, Matthew," Lester said into the bullhorn.

"So, his name is really Matthew," Livy had never known the man to be anything other than Butter Bean.

"We can work this out if you'll just come down here," the portly officer-of-the-peace said through the squelching horn.

The hardware store was only one story tall so Livy questioned whether or not Butter Bean could have really committed suicide, but Lester was treating him as if a fall from the twelve-foot building would surely be fatal.

"I can't come down," Butter Bean wailed. "I just can't," he cried, tears streaming down his cheeks.

Livy was also about to cry, sure that everyone who had butter beaned him for years, had finally pushed him over the edge.

"Why not?" Lester interrupted her remorseful examination. "Look no matter what the problem is, it seems worse than it really is. I promise," he pleaded some more.

Butter Bean tried to convince Lester that it was indeed the end of the world. "No! It *is* really bad. It doesn't just seem like it's bad. It really, really is!"

"Somebody go 'n get Mrs. Wallup," Lester said to the crowd.

Mrs. Wallup was Butter Bean's mother who apparently did not know of the episode unfolding at the appliance store.

"No!" Butter Bean shouted at the crowd. "Don't get my mother! My mother is the one I'm afraid of!" he cried. "She is just going to kill me for what I've done!"

"Now, now, Matthew, your mother is not going to kill you," Lester reasoned.

Livy had to agree. Butter Bean's mother was a tiny, little dumpling of a lady that was so incredibly sweet, she could win a dessert contest just by showing up. In fact, she was one of Livy's favorite customers. The woman often came into the drugstore to get her prescriptions. While she waited, she would shyly ask Livy to make her a vanilla malt. Livy thought she had the most beautiful and friendly smile she had ever seen. Livy had never seen a more adorable old person, and it made her want to squeeze the precious woman.

"I don't want you to get my mother!" Butter Bean pleaded, snapping Livy back to the events unfolding across the street. "This is just going to upset her! It's just better if I end things right now!" He stepped closer to the edge of the roof.

"Matthew, I will not let you jump off this building!" The panic in Lester's voice was clear. "I can help you if you'll just let me."

"How can you help me?" Butter Bean began crying again. "Nobody can fix this!" He sobbed, shaking his round and fat head.

Listening to the exchange, Livy began to believe that Butter Bean's problems had nothing to do with her or her friends. She sighed in relief.

"It's too late. I'm too far along," Butter Bean yelled down at the rotund policeman.

"No, you're not Matthew! And it's never too late," Lester was not sure why it may be too late, but nevertheless, he disagreed with the disheartened jumper.

"Even after three months?" Butter Bean cocked his head to one side, a glimmer of hope taking place.

Lester hesitated. "Um, yes, even after three months," he looked around at the crowd, trying to see if they were as bewildered as he was.

"Are you sure?" Butter Bean asked again, stepping back a little from the edge.

"Absolutely, I'm sure," Lester saw the exchange was working, and he called on help from the crowd. "We're all sure, aren't we?"

"Uh huh," came the unanimous, but befuddled, reply.

It was then that Mrs. Wallup came shuffling up the sidewalk. Boomer Daws had her by the elbow helping her to navigate the uneven pavement.

"Matthew," she said when she arrived at the tan brick building and looked up to see her son, "what are you doing up there, precious?"

Livy almost melted in her shoes at the sweetness of the old woman.

"I'm sorry, Mama," Butter Bean, got a look of complete heartbreak on his face and began to cry again. "I'm in big trouble and I didn't want you to find out about it. I didn't want to hurt you." He mournfully sobbed.

"Oh, Matthew," the darling woman sighed. "You could never hurt me; don't you know that?" Her face implored him to realize the depth of her love. "You are my little man, and there is nothing you could ever do that would hurt me so badly that I would want you gone." A tear slipped down her cheek.

"Matthew," she beseeched, "the only thing you could do to hurt me would be to leave me."

Most of the crowd now had tears of their own wetting their cheeks.

Butter Bean sniffled. "But Mama," he sighed, begging his mother to realize the gravity of the situation, "I'm pregnant."

Tears stopped, the crowd froze, and no one took a breath.

The bullhorn fell to Lester's side, dangling while he processed what the eccentric man had just revealed. Once he had, he placed the bullhorn back to his lips.

"You're pregnant?" he asked, knowing he could not have heard the man correctly. "You mean like you're going to have a baby?" he furrowed his paunchy forehead.

"Uh huh," Butter Bean said, nodding his head up and down.

"Oh my," Mrs. Wallup said, putting a hand to her cheek.

"Did he say he was pregnant?" Livy heard someone behind her ask.

"That's sure enough what he said," someone else answered.

"Oh my God," was the next remark.

Lester lowered the bullhorn and looked at Mrs. Wallup. "Do you want to tell him, or should I?"

Mrs. Wallup bit her lip and looked at the ground, obviously embarrassed. "I'll tell him," she whispered.

"Matthew?" Lester hollered to him without the use of the bullhorn. "You come on down now. Everything is okay. Your mama's gonna' take you home."

Butter Bean wiped his nose on his shirtsleeve and sniffed a couple of times. He backed away from the edge one step at a time until he was a good ten feet away. Then, he turned and walked to the back of the store and onto the ladder from which he had made his ascent. He struggled, and wobbled, and prissed his butt out. It was then that Livy realized that the other gay guy in town that Michael had mentioned, and who indeed wasn't tall dark or handsome, was Butter Bean. And that meant that he was Michael's cousin.

Lester turned back to the crowd.

"Ya'll go on back to your stores now," he ordered. "Ain't nothin' else here for you to see."

The crowd began dispersing but not quietly.

"Sweet Lord in Heaven," Livy heard Mrs. Doodle say. "That boy thinks he is with child."

"Well if he is, we are going to make the TV news," Ralph said. "We'll have a real bona fide miracle on our hands, won't we?" He laughed while jabbing Morty in the ribs.

"Poor Mrs. Wallup," Livy said to Ethel. "She's so sweet."

"Well, you think she would have taught that boy about the birds and the bees," Barbara interjected.

"That's what we pay the school for," Livy's mom answered.

Barbara nodded her agreement.

"Oh, gosh," Ethel cut in. "There's nobody at the store." She slapped her head, before taking off back down the sidewalk.

Mary Ann called after her. "Don't hurt yourself, Ethel. Everyone in town is up here."

The rest of the crowd dispersed to their separate destinations, as the four remaining women walked slowly back to the drugstore. They were each lost in their own thoughts, which were all the same. How did Butter Bean ever get the idea that he was pregnant?

Chapter Twenty-Four

The Questioning

As the group neared the store, Livy saw the two OSBI agents crossing the street from the police station. Curly waved, motioning to her. Livy's mother looked at them, then her daughter.

"Who are those guys?" she asked the girl suspiciously.

"They were in the store earlier today having coffee," Livy explained. "They're those Oklahoma City police guys that are helping Lester with the robberies."

"Oh," Mary Ann replied, looking from them back to Livy. "Well, why are they waving at you?" she interrogated as if she was about to find out that the girl was a hardened criminal.

"Because I told them about when Granny Stephens almost got robbed."

Mary Ann's face reddened. "Why did you go and do something stupid like that?" she asked.

Livy did not understand the hostility. "What's so stupid about telling them?"

"You don't need to go sticking your nose in where it doesn't belong," her mother admonished. "You're just going to get yourself into trouble. Besides, they get paid to find things out. They don't need some teenage kid telling them how to do their job."

"Geez, So Sorry!" Livy raised her voice and pouted.

The two were almost to the storefront, and Mary Ann made sure they could both hear her next remark.

"You hurry up and get your butt in the store. We'll be closing in a few hours, and you have a lot to get done," she threatened while keeping her eyes on the agents. As they stepped up onto the sidewalk, she turned and went inside.

"Miss Stephens," Curly said. "Is there any way you could take us to see your grandmother. It'll only take a minute," he added, addressing her mother's warning.

"Uh… I guess so," Livy reluctantly agreed, "but we have to hurry because if I don't get my stuff done, I can't go to the Toilet Bowl tonight."

The two men looked at each other. "Don't even go there," Glasses said to Curly, who nodded his understanding.

"Okay." Curly exhaled. "Our car is right across the street. We'll get you back in a jiffy. Do you want to tell your mom you're going?"

"No way," Livy shook her head. "If I tell her, I'll for sure be in trouble. Let's just go and get back before she knows I'm gone."

Livy slid into the backseat of the large, black unmarked car. She began checking it out. The front dashboard had a radio that looked like a CB and a panel of buttons that normal cars didn't have. It also had a big dome looking red and blue light lying on the seat next to a large pistol. The girl reached for it, but not before Glasses slapped her hand.

"What do you think you are doing girl?" he admonished.

"Ouch! Hey that hurt," Livy griped, pulling back her hand.

"Good, it was supposed to," the detective countered.

"I just wanted to see it," Livy whined.

"Lady, a man's gun is sacred," the obviously annoyed detective declared. "Don't you ever grab anyone's gun again, you hear?" He huffed before calming back down. "Besides, it's dangerous, you could have killed one of us."

"Not likely unless I really wanted to," Livy boasted. "I've had a gun in my hands since I was knee high. My dad and my brothers and I always shoot. I have a Twenty-gage shot gun of my own." Livy was gloating. "And," she added sarcastically, "I have Colt Detective Special that my daddy got me to take to college when I go. He got it because it's hammerless and it won't go off in my purse..." she stopped, realizing that they might have the same gun.

"You guys are detectives! Do you have Detective Speicals too?"

Glasses looked at Curly again in disbelief. "Who in the hell are these people?" he asked.

Curly laughed. "Welcome to rural Oklahoma, buddy."

Livy directed the two to her grandmother's house. When they pulled into the driveway, she issued a warning.

"Now, you two just stay here until I let her know who it is. Only when I tell you, can you come in," she relayed while exiting the car.

Livy climbed the three steps of the old, gray, wooden porch and knocked on the door.

"Granny, it's me," she yelled.

"Just a minute, I'm on my way," she heard her grandmother answer.

The white wooden door opened revealing a small, thin woman, with salt and pepper hair cut into a pageboy. The unpretentious woman was wearing a blue flowered housecoat and white house slippers.

The homeowner looked at Livy through the metal and glass storm door and smiled.

"Just a minute here, and let me get this thing open," she fiddled with the door, her arthritic fingers fumbling with the lock.

Livy didn't wait for her grandmother to open the door before explaining why she was there. "Granny, I have two guys here that want to talk to you. They are helping Lester try and solve the robberies. Can they come in?"

Maudie Stephens finally managed the locks and pushed open the door.

"Well, I guess," she hesitated. "But I don't have on anything but my house coat. I'm not really dressed for company."

"It's okay," Livy said motioning to the detectives. "You look just fine."

The two exited the car while Mrs. Stephens sized them up. Curly brushed past Glasses and bounded up the steps.

"Hi Mrs. Stephens," he said, sticking out his hand to shake hers.

Livy's granny awkwardly shook his hand while still eyeing Glasses.

"I'm Agent Douglas, and this is my partner, Agent Brett. We are with the Oklahoma State Bureau of Investigation," he informed her.

"Oh goodness me," Livy's granny, now obviously intimidated, said backing away. "I really don't know anything." She crossly looked at her granddaughter, her face asking her why she had gotten her involved.

Livy tried to redeem herself and at the same time calm her grandmother's nerves. "Granny, I already told them about the two ladies that tried to use your phone. They just want to ask you about that. You're not in trouble or anything," she said, trying to reassure her.

"Well I don't know any more than what I told you," she said, acting very uncomfortable. Livy nudged Curly, trying to get him to calm the woman.

"Mrs. Stephens, we just wanted to ask you a couple of things. Your granddaughter told us you might recognize one of the women and that you thought you may have seen her recently," he said smiling.

Mrs. Stephens took a deep breath, resigning herself to the request before motioning for the three to come in.

Livy's granny took a seat on small glider rocker and pointed the detectives toward her light-yellow vinyl sofa.

"Mrs. Stephens," Curly began before he had even sat down, "Livy says you think you may have seen one of the women last night."

Livy's granny bit her lower lip. "Well, I'm not exactly sure," she answered. "But there was a woman over at Mrs. Spivey's last night that sure looked a lot like the older one that had come here. But I couldn't say for sure." "It was dark," she added.

Livy could see, because of her grandmother's reluctance to get involved, that she was downplaying what she had seen. Her grandmother was not one to be unsure of anything. And if she said she saw something, then she saw it.

"What did this woman look like, Mrs. Stephens," Glasses inquired.

"She was fat," the woman answered, matter of fact.

"Is that all, just heavy?" Glasses pushed for more information.

"Well, no," Livy's granny rolled her eyes, not appreciating being patronized. "She was fat. She had bleached blond, greasy hair, and she needed a dye job."

Livy squelched a giggle.

"Was her hair short or long?" Glasses ignored the woman's curtness.

"Neither," Mrs. Stephens stated.

"Neither?" Glasses raised his eyebrows, trying again to coax the woman into a longer answer.

"Nope, it wasn't short and it wasn't long," she told the unvarnished truth.

Frustrated, Glasses looked at Curly. "I see where this one gets it," he said pointing to Livy. Livy's grandmother looked at her granddaughter, unsure if she should be offended.

"I'm sorry Mrs. Stephens," Curly ignored his partner. "Could you be more specific?"

"Yep," the woman replied. "It was about to here," she said using her hand to make a sawing motion across her shoulders. "Longer than mine," she added.

"So, it was shoulder length then?" Curly quizzed.

"Yep, and it was real greasy like it hadn't been washed in a month of Sundays."

"You said that you saw her last night across the street. What was she doing?" Curly continued his inquiry.

"I don't know," the petite lady shrugged. "She was just standing there."

"Do you think she was one of Mrs. Spivey's son's wives?" Curly asked.

"No. I know their wives, and none of the girls were there. Just two of her sons."

"So, she was just standing there?" Glasses broke in.

"Yeah, just watching the funeral guy take Mrs. Spivey," Granny said.

"Do you think she might just be a neighbor new to the street or one close by?" he queried.

"No, she doesn't live on this street. We do have new neighbors down at Mrs. Teener's old place, but I've met them. They actually check up on me quite frequently. Nice people."

"Was there anyone else there that you didn't recognize?" Glasses asked.

"No, just her," Livy's granny replied.

Both agents looked at each other long and hard. Curly was twisting his mouth to one side like he was deep in thought. "Strange," he finally said, getting out of his seat. "Well I guess, that will about do it."

Glasses added. "We want to thank you for your time, Mrs. Stephens. You have been very helpful. If it's okay with you, we might want to come back at some point and show you a picture of the perpetrators to help us identify them."

Livy's granny obviously knew the meaning of perpetrator because she told the detective that would be fine.

As the two agents walked out the front door, Livy stayed behind to give her granny a hug.

"I hope they didn't scare you, Granny," she apologized.

"Nope, it would take a lot more than two wet behind the ears city slicker policemen to scare me," Mrs. Stephens replied, although Livy could sense she was a little on edge.

"I love you," the girl smiled, as she hugged the woman who was now at least five inches shorter than her.

"Love you too, Sweetie," she responded. "Come have pie with me tomorrow."

Livy grinned. "You know I can't turn down your pic, Granny." I'll see you tomorrow," she said, as she closed the door. Then she stopped, looked over her shoulder, and hollered. "Lock the door Granny."

Click. It was locked.

Chapter Twenty-Five

One Step Closer

As Livy opened the car door to get in, Curly looked at Glasses, "Why would there be a woman who's not a part of the family, not a neighbor, and not with the funeral home standing around watching?" he asked his partner.

"Probably best that we save this conversation for later," Glasses turned to look at Livy.

Livy seeing they were excluding her, protested. "Hey! You can talk in front of me I won't tell anyone," she promised.

"That's not the way it works, Livy," Curly answered flatly. "Our investigations are confidential until they are solved, and even then, some parts remain confidential."

"Well, just tell me this. Do you think my Granny saw a woman at Mrs. Spivey's or do you think she was mistaken because of the dark and all?"

"Don't know," Curly shrugged. "But we have to check it out. That's our job. Who did you say worked at the funeral home that picked up, Mrs. Spivey?" He looked into the rearview mirror again at the girl.

"My friend Michael works there. But another guy, Richy, was the one who picked her up."

"And you say this Richy person has already said he didn't take anyone with him?" he questioned.

"That's what Michael said," Livy responded.

"Do you know if Richy is working today?" Glasses took over the questioning.

"Yeah, Michael said he was."

"Well, we will drop you off and go have a chat with your friends," Curly imparted.

The detective pulled up next to the drugstore and double-parked behind two cars that were parked in front.

"Thanks for your help with Mrs. Stephens," Curly turned to look at Livy as she got out of the car.

"No problem," Livy exited before sticking her head back in. "You guys were really nice to her, but remember, if you do go back to see her, take me with you. I don't want her to be scared."

"Will do," Curly assured.

Livy shut the door and watched the car ease away. The men drove to the First Baptist Church then made a U-turn heading back toward the funeral home. Livy couldn't wait to tell Michael they were on their way, so she sprinted into the store and straight to the phone.

"Michael," she said as soon as he answered the phone, "the OBI guys are on their way to talk to you and Richy. They will be there any second!" Livy could barely contain her excitement.

"Okay," Michael nonchalantly replied. "And it's OSBI," he corrected her again.

Livy ignored his correction. "Aren't you worried? Aren't you scared?" she asked, trying to get him to realize the monumental significance of the moment.

"No. I told you we talk to them all the time on unattended deaths," he responded, acting very bored with her.

"Fine," Livy huffed, mad that he wasn't impressed with being part of the once-in-a-lifetime investigation. "Oh," she added, trying to get a rise out of him in a different manner, "why didn't you tell me that Butter Bean was your cousin?"

"Ohhhhh," she heard the abject horror in Michael's voice, and it made her smile.

"How did you find that out?" he gasped.

Livy was thrilled, finally getting the rise she had been looking for.

"Let's just say I recognized the family resemblance," she taunted.

"You are such a … Oh, they're here," Michael interrupted his thought. "Got to go." He hung up on her.

Livy was disappointed that her torment couldn't continue, but then Ethel interrupted her.

"What's all that about," she asked, searching Livy's face for a clue.

"Oh nothing," Livy replied, trying to avoid another lecture about how she should stay out of other people's business.

"In that case, it's time for you to start mopping up," Ethel directed. "I'll get started on cleaning the fountain. With any luck, we can get out of here a bit early tonight." Ethel yawned, showing the wear of the day.

Livy hated having to sweep and mop the floor. She thought she was way too sophisticated to act as a janitor. She piddled on her way back to retrieve the mop and bucket, trying to delay the demeaning task as long as possible. When she reached the pharmacy, she let her disgust be known, as she had done at least a million times before.

"Why can't Sam come and mop?" she whined as she passed her mother.

"Because he's at football," Mary Ann replied.

"Yeah, well he could come in tomorrow and do it," she whined some more.

"If he comes in tomorrow, that means that I have to come in tomorrow and Sundays are my only day off. I don't want to come in. Now stop complaining and mop!" she said, pointing a finger to the back of the store where the mop and bucket were kept.

"Football, football, football," Livy moaned under her breath. "It's not fair. I have to work my butt off all day, and he gets to play football." Livy managed to conveniently put out of her mind the two-a-day summer practices in 100 plus degree temperatures, and the practices every night until dark that her brothers had to endure. She rolled the heavy mop bucket up to the soda tables where she began stacking the chairs on top so she could mop underneath.

Ethel interrupted Livy's self-absorbed complaining.

"What kind of surprise should we leave for Alberta on Monday?" Ethel snickered from behind the fountain.

Livy stopped a moment to think. "How 'bout an animal cracker under the grates?" she said pointing to the wooden slats beneath Ethel's feet.

"Animal cracker it is," Ethel agreed, grabbing a bag from the potato chip rack and tearing into them.

She held the bag up to show Livy. "Elephant or monkey?"

Livy smirked. "Elephant and monkey! The more, the better!"

Ethel stooped over to place the crackers under the grate. She left just a fraction hanging out the side so Alberta couldn't miss it when she opened on Monday. "There. Two hissy-fit instigating Animal Crackers."

The phone rang, and Ethel reached to answer it.

"Stephens' Drug," she said. "Just a minute," she sounded annoyed. "Livy, it's for you again. You need to make it quick and get this place cleaned up so we can go home soon," she shook her finger at the teen.

"I will," Livy agreed, grabbing the phone. "Heeeellllloooo!" She tried to sound like Count Chocula.

"You're not going to believe this," Michael whispered.

"Why are you whispering?" Livy whispered back.

"Because those agents are still here. They just finished talking to Mr. Winters, and they're about to leave. I don't want them to hear me," he explained, his voice becoming even quieter.

"Really?" Livy was getting excited. "What did they want? What did they say? Do they have any suspects? Are you and Richy going to jail?"

"Stop! Just shut up and listen. They came in here and asked to talk to Richy. They talked to him in the front parlor so I overheard everything," Michael reported. "They wanted to know if there was a girl with him last night at Mrs. Spivey's – just like you did. He told them that there wasn't; that he had picked her up alone. Then they asked him if there was any girl there last night, and he told them no. They finished talking with Richy and were getting ready to leave, but then Richy turned around and told them to wait a minute because he did remember something."

Livy was so charged she couldn't stand still. Ethel eyed her wondering if she had to pee.

"Then," Michael continued, "he leaned in real close to the tall one and whispered something to him. I couldn't hear what it was, but the agents both looked at each other and then asked if they could speak to Mr. Winters," Michael stopped to take a breath and see what Livy had to say.

"Yeah? Yeah? Yeah?" Livy coaxed.

"They talked to him a minute..." Livy heard the phone become muffled. "Hang on a minute," Michael whispered. Livy waited anxiously before he continued. "Now they are leaving, and they are taking Richy with them." The phone muffled again, Michael obviously had covered it with his hand. Livy was getting more anxious by the second.

"Oh my gosh," Michael said as he put the receiver back to his mouth. "As they were going out the door, I heard one of them say to the other that they would need to have a sit down with Lester. They are on their way back to the police station."

"Oooooh, you think they have figured it out and are on their way to tell Lester who it is?" Livy hopped up and down with excitement.

Ethel walked in front of her and pointed to her watch. Livy nodded.

"Could be," Michael reasoned.

"Okay, I've got to go. But you make sure you call me if you hear anything else, understand?" she ordered.

"I will," Michael promised before hanging up.

Livy went to the front door and watched the black car pass the drugstore. It again went to the church and made a U-turn coming back down the street before pulling into City Hall.

Both the agents and Richy got out and walked up the front steps, disappearing inside.

Livy reluctantly went back to mopping. As she swished the big twine mop back and forth across the floor, she let her mind wander to what might be taking place across the street. Who would the two lawmen arrest for the robbing spree? Was it someone they all knew or was it some unknown stranger who had just been passing through? Had Livy's granny really seen the woman last night, or was it just her old eyes failing her? Livy was beginning to imagine a huge shootout, the kind that she'd seen on television.

In her version, the two agents would come barreling out of the police station, one jumping over the hood of their car to get to his door, the other diving through the window. Then they would go screeching down the street, sirens wailing. They would pull up to a house or even better, a store. They'd swing the doors of the car open, guns drawn and yell "Freeze! You're under arrest!" to a big mean woman who was wielding a huge knife and threatening them with every step they took.

"Livy, what is going on in that head of yours?" Ethel broke right into the middle of her Oscar Award winning scene. "I've been hollering at you for five minutes. You need to move that doormat and mop under it. It gets sticky because people are always spilling stuff on it," Ethel pointed at the front door.

"Okay," Livy huffed, annoyed that Ethel butted into her action-packed drama.

Livy looked back out the door and across the street. Lester's wife and daughter were pulling into a parking spot, making one of their frequent visits to see Lester. They got out their old beat up El Camino, and like the agents before them, climbed the two steps into City Hall, before disappearing inside.

Livy looked at the clock. It was getting close to four. The store would close at five and then she could go home and get ready for the Toilet Bowl. Hopefully, she would walk Mitch off the field. Livy finished the mopping, taking the bucket out back to be emptied.

It was then she realized that she never called Stevy back to give her permission to call Brandon. She had secretly wanted her to do it, but she needed to protest in case Mitch said no. That way at least she could save herself some embarrassment and say she never wanted her friend to ask in the first place. Livy was still hesitant to give her the go ahead, but her huge crush overshadowed her ego. She picked up the phone that was in the back storeroom and dialed.

"Hello?" a dull and deep voice answered. It was Stevy's little brother, Craig. "Hey Q-Tip," she said to the burly cotton headed kid, who was as much a little brother to her as her own. "Let me talk to Stevy," she ordered the boy who she had nicknamed for a cotton swab.

He grunted and laid the phone down. "Stevy, get the phone. It's your evil twin," Livy heard him yell. While it was true they had similar haircuts and were both blond, Livy didn't appreciate being dubbed the evil one.

"Hey," she started to protest, but Stevy had already picked up the receiver.

"I was wondering if you were ever going to call me back. It may be too late to call Mitch," she said in a duh sort of way. "Brandon said they had to be at the field house by four. Do you want me to see if you can walk him off?"

"I guess," Livy sighed. "But DON'T tell Brandon that I wanted you to ask," she threatened. "I mean it, Stevy. Just act like it was all your idea," she threatened again.

"Livy, I know how to do this." Livy could tell she was rolling her eyes.

"Okay, call me back when you're done. And DON'T tell Brandon I asked you to!"

Stevy hung up on her.

Livy decided to make a quick stop at the rest room, before checking with Ethel to see if she needed help to finish cleaning the fountain.

As she came back into the main part of the store, she saw Curly and Glasses coming through the front door again. They stopped at the fountain and talked to Ethel while Livy made her way toward them. She saw Ethel pointing to her.

"Livy," Curly said, as she approached. "We need to speak to your grandmother again."

Ethel cocked her head and looked at Livy, her stares asking what the heck was going on.

Livy avoided her gaze and cleared her throat, trying to whisper so she wouldn't alert her mother. "Umm…okay, I guess," she stammered.

Ethel now had her hands on her hips and her lips pursed, warning Livy that she was just seconds from calling Mary Ann to the front.

"It's okay, Ethel," Livy lied. "Mom already knows. They are from Oklahoma City, and they are helping Lester with the old folk's robberies. My Granny Stephens saw the women who did it, and they were just asking her questions."

Ethel seemed satisfied with the answer and continued her cleaning chores, still shooting Livy glances from time to time.

"Can you go with us really quickly?" Glasses asked. "It will take us less than ten minutes," he justified, looking to Ethel.

"Is it okay, Ethel?" Livy asked.

"I'm sure it is," she replied. "Mopping is done and the fountain is pretty much cleaned."

"Okay, if Mom asks, tell her I'll be right back," Livy said as she grabbed her denim purse from behind the counter.

The trio crossed the almost deserted street and got into the unmarked car. This time, the gun was nowhere to be seen.

"We have suspects," Curly revealed, as he stretched his long legs under the steering wheel.

"You do?" Livy bounced up and down a little in her seat from the excitement. "Who?"

"That's confidential," Glasses shook his head like he had had all of the girl he cared to deal with for one day.

"We just need to show your grandmother a picture we have. As I said before, it will only take a few minutes," Curly reiterated over his shoulder while backing out.

When they got to Mrs. Stephens' house, Livy repeated the same process as before. She went to the door first to talk to her grandmother. Livy could tell that she did not want to go through it all again but, reluctantly, she let the officers in.

"Sorry to bother you again Mrs. Stephens," Curly apologized, as he pulled a manila envelope from inside his coat. "We think we know who the women may be who have been robbing senior citizens. We have a picture here and would like you to take a look at it."

Granny nodded her head. "That was fast," she was surprised at how quickly the men had come back.

"Well, it kind of fell into our laps," Glasses shrugged. "Really can't take much credit for it."

Curly pulled a 5 x 7 picture from the envelope and showed it to Livy's grandmother.

"You know I said that I *thought* we had found the women – and I do – but if this isn't them, please don't hesitate to tell us. You don't have to say the women in the picture are them if they aren't," he clarified. "It won't hurt our feelings. We've been wrong before." He bent down to try to look into her eyes.

"I know that." She brushed him away, feeling patronized. "I would never say somebody did something if they didn't."

She looked at the photo for less than a split second. "That's them," she said shaking her head up and down. "It sure is."

"Are you sure," Glasses asked, "You didn't look very long."

"Didn't have to," the woman replied, looking up at him. "I'd know that bad bleach job anywhere, and now that I've seen them when I'm not scared, I can tell you who it is too!" She pointed her finger in the air for emphasis.

"We know who it is," Curly said. "We know exactly who it is."

"Well good!" Livy's grandmother was showing some excitement at the whole unfolding drama. "I hope you take the proper care of those two." She clicked the dentures in her mouth. "How dare they do that to old folks. Especially them!"

Livy was about to pee her pants waiting for someone to tell her who had been terrorizing the little town, but it appeared that everyone had forgotten that she even existed. Just as she started to protest, Glasses interrupted.

"We appreciate you very much, Mrs. Stephens. We wouldn't have been able to crack this without you. You have been more than helpful," he said, turning to leave.

Curly shook Mrs. Stephens' hand and turned away as well. "Come on Livy, we have to get back to the police station before we lose our suspects."

"Huh?" Livy answered, but the two men were already out the door leaving her no time to ask her granny who it was. "I'll call you in a minute," she hollered back to her grandmother as Curly waved her to get a move-on. "Lock your door," she yelled as she hit the last step.

Chapter Twenty-Six

It All Falls Into Place

As soon the three got into the car Livy began pummeling them with questions. "Who did it? What did Granny mean, 'especially them?' How do you know who *they* are? Are *they* wanted all over? Are *they* famous criminals? Will somebody PLEASE just tell me something?!" she exhaled in a most theatrical fashion.

Glasses shook his head, refusing to even acknowledge Livy. Curly looked at her in the rearview mirror. "Livy, we've been over this before. It's con-fi-den-tial," he said, stating each syllable as if it was its own word.

"Arrrrgh!" she slammed her body back into the seat. "That's not fair!" she protested. "I helped you! I helped both of you! I should at the very least be told what is going on! I deserve that!" She hit her fist against the seat so they would see how serious she was.

"Sorry kid, not today," Curly ignored her hysterics.

Livy, sullen, stared out the window for the two-minute drive to the store. The car pulled into a spot in front, and Curly turned to look at the surly girl. He tried placating her. "Listen, Livy, we really do appreciate your help. You were important to this case, and just like your grandma, we couldn't have done it without you."

Livy, however, was not about to let him off the hook. She glared at her curly headed enemy while opening the door. She continued to glare as she slammed it shut. Glasses paid no attention to her while Curly shook his head as he backed out.

Seeing she was having no effect, Livy turned and ran into the drugstore to call her grandmother. Even if she couldn't get those too-big-for-their-britches detectives to tell her what was going on, she knew she could get her granny to do it.

Livy ran for the phone and picked it up. As fate would have it, her mother was on the extension in the pharmacy talking to a customer.

"Dang, dang, dang, dang, dang, dang, dang!" she said to herself while replacing the receiver.

Ethel rounded the fountain, listening to Livy's rant, but thought better than to get involved. Instead, she ordered the girl to get more soda cups from the storage area in the back.

"Dang, dang, dang, dang, dang, dang, dang!" she said to herself again realizing the chore would delay her call even more.

Livy huffed and clenched her teeth all the way to the back supply shelves. Barbara stuck her head through the door as Livy searched for the cups. "Ethel said to get more coffee cups too," she relayed.

"Fine," Livy huffed again while moving boxes around in search of them. She played over in her head the conversation her grandmother had with the detectives.

"Who is 'especially them?" she asked herself, but had no answer.

Livy found the cups and grabbed two sleeves of each. As she opened the storage room door, she saw Ethel standing at the front talking with Thelma Horton, the City Clerk, whose office was right across the hall from the police dispatcher's.

Thelma had the whitest blondest hair Livy had ever seen. It was piled up on top of her head in an excessively high beehive. The woman also loved to wear lipstick that more resembled white correction fluid instead of lip color. Her hair and lipstick made the clerk appear almost ghostly.

Thelma was waving her arms and talking a mile a minute to Ethel. Ethel was shaking her head up and down like she was agreeing and then shaking her head back and forth like she was disagreeing. Livy made haste to the front of the store when she saw Ethel clasp her hand over her mouth in disbelief.

"Can you imagine?" Thelma was saying when Livy arrived. "I mean it, Ethel, can you?" she repeated.

Ethel was still standing with her hand over her mouth shaking her head no.

"Who would have ever believed this? I mean I wouldn't have believed it unless I had seen it with my own eyes and heard it with my own ears. Doesn't this just beat all? I mean really, Ethel, doesn't it?" she reiterated.

Ethel had removed her hand and was now shaking her head yes. Livy could stand it no more.

"What? What beats all?" she interrupted.

Thelma ignored the girl and continued her discourse. "I wonder what this is going to mean for me?" Thelma put her own hand over her mouth. "I mean I didn't have anything to do with it that's for sure," She pleaded her unknown case to Ethel.

Livy tried again. "What's going to affect you?" she asked louder.

Ethel shooed Livy away – at least she tried to. However, the girl was not about to move one inch until she learned of the latest debacle in a day of debacles.

"When did this happen?" Ethel finally spoke.

"Just now," Thelma answered, becoming excited again. "I mean just two minutes ago. I couldn't stand to watch anymore. I just had to leave. I saw you over here, so I thought I would make a quick getaway."

"Oh my," Ethel shook her head some more, "I just can't believe it, Thelma. Really, I can't."

"BELIEVE WHAT?!" Livy yelled. "What can't you believe, Ethel?"

Ethel turned in exasperation to the teenager. "You need to mind your P's and Q's," she scolded. "Now go get your mother."

Livy stood there and blinked

"Now!" she commanded.

"Why?" What's wrong? Just tell me!" Livy pleaded to no avail.

"Go!" Ethel ordered her again, pointing to the pharmacy.

Livy finally conceded running to the back and sticking her head inside the pharmacy.

"Mom, Ethel needs you quick," she relayed.

Mary Ann sensed her daughter's urgency and jumped from her stool. She bounded down the step of the pharmacy booth and headed toward the front. Barbara, overhearing the exchange, followed after, alerting Lucy on her way. The two women followed Mary Ann to the front of the store.

"Mary Ann," Ethel stated, as soon as she and the rest of the women approached. "They arrested the people who tried to rob your mother-in-law."

"Really? Who was it?"

"Are you ready for this?" Ethel tried to prepare the clerks.

"Who?" Mary Ann demanded.

"It was Lester's wife and daughter!" Ethel watched the women's reaction with great interest.

"What?" Mary Ann took a swaying step backward. "You have got to be kidding me? How in the world could Lester let them do something like that?" the woman questioned.

"Lester didn't know," Thelma interrupted. "He was just as shocked as everyone when the OSBI agents arrested them a minute ago. Apparently, because they always knew where Lester would be, it made it easy for them to operate. I'm sure if he had of known, he would have never called those agents."

"Your mother-in-law and the boy down at the funeral home are the ones who figured it out," Ethel jumped in.

"My mother-in-law?" Mary Ann asked, completely confused.

"Yeah, she saw Lester's wife helping him take the body of Mrs. Spivey last night, and she recognized her. She told the OSBI agents, and they talked to the boy at the funeral home about who was there last night. They asked him if there were any women at Mrs. Spivey's, and he told them no. But then he remembered Lester's wife," Thelma said.

Thelma went on to explain how it wasn't uncommon for Lester's wife to go on coroner calls with Lester, and how Richy said he had never really thought of Patsy, Lester's wife, as a girl.

"He always just kind of thought of her as some big, ol' whatever," Thelma continued. "But when everyone kept asking him about a girl being there last night, he realized that even though he thought of her as just a big whatever, that she was really a woman and he told the agents!"

"Unbelievable," was all Mary Ann could say.

Thelma continued unraveling the saga for the group. "Those agents saw a picture of Patsy and the daughter, Marsha, on Lester's desk. They realized she matched your mother-in-law's description." She turned to Mary Ann. "They didn't tell Lester why, but they asked him to have both the women come down just to answer some routine questions."

"Unbelievable," Barbara echoed.

"Apparently, the agents came over here and got your girl," Thelma pointed to Livy. Mary Ann's eyes bugged from her head as she snapped her head to glare at Livy.

Livy tried to disappear when luckily Thelma took off again with the story and her mother's head popped back to the ghostly woman.

"When they came back from wherever it was they went with your daughter..." Mary Ann's head popped back to Livy along with the bugged eyes and an added scowl, "they brought Patsy and Marsha with them to the meeting room to talk," she continued. "Annnnd," she drew the word out for extra emphasis, "they wouldn't let Lester in."

Thelma reported that at first, Lester didn't seem to mind and he went back to his office. "I tell you, he really had no idea it was them!" she nodded. "Pretty soon, Patsy started yelling, and Lester went down to see what was going on. The agents told him he couldn't be there, and that's when he got upset and wouldn't leave." Thelma looked around at the group to make sure they were following the story.

"Anyway, when Lester refused to leave, they threatened to charge him with obstruction of justice!" She stamped her foot, in a "doesn't that beat all?" gesture.

"Did he leave?" Barbara asked.

"Yeah, but he stood outside the door listening, and I joined him there so I could hear too," she confessed. "Then the girl started to cry and Lester couldn't stand it. He opened the door and demanded the agents tell him what was going on. That's when he found out what had happened."

"That can't be," Lucy said in disbelief.

"Oh yes, it can," Thelma contradicted. "Lester begged Patsy to tell the detectives it wasn't true. She wouldn't, and that's when she finally confessed! She said she and Marsha had been the ones robbing people! She said Lester didn't make enough money and she wanted to help out." Thelma slapped her hand against her thigh.

"After Patsy and Marsha confessed, the agents arrested both of them!" she slapped her thigh once again. "Lester just broke down crying his eyes out and asking them both 'Why?' over and over. He kept saying that they didn't need any more money than they already had, but Patsy told him he was wrong. She said, 'Your daughter needs all the things that the other rich little girls in town have.'"

"Well I'll be a monkey's uncle," Barbara piped up again. "Our policeman's wife and daughter. Who would have ever thought it?"

Mary Ann looked at the ceiling deep in thought. "What rich little girls?" she inquired, obviously confused. "His daughter is almost thirty, and besides, there are NO rich little girls of any age in this entire town."

The group was quiet for a moment, letting the newly unfolded events take root, until Mary Ann broke the silence.

"How did my mother-in-law get involved in this?" she accusingly turned toward Livy.

"Don't know," Thelma answered, much to Livy's relief. "Doesn't matter though. She was right. She's pretty sharp for someone her age," Thelma inadvertently agreed with Livy's assessment of the woman. "And I guess it's lucky that the funeral home boy remembered Lester's wife," she added.

It finally all made sense to Livy why her grandmother had recognized Lester's wife and daughter from the picture. The two had previously worked at the city's public swimming pool and her grandmother had taken Sam and her there to swim on several occasions. She must not have recognized them when they tried to rob her because it had been several years since she had seen them. The picture that Lester had on his desk was probably taken back when they looked more like what her grandmother would have remembered.

"Well, I guess I better get back over there," Thelma said, looking across the street. "Lester's not going to know what to do with himself. He was still bawling like a little baby when I left, and I can't believe it, but I feel sorry for him."

"Yeah," Ethel agreed, "he will never live it down that he couldn't catch the culprits when they were right under his very own roof."

Thelma turned to leave and Ethel looked at Mary Ann.

"You okay?" she asked.

"Yes." Mary Ann, answered while watching Thelma reluctantly return to City Hall. "I guess I better call Lenard," she stated, referring to Livy's father. "He'll want to go check on his mother."

Barbara, Lucy, and Mary Ann returned to the back of the store.

"You through with your chores?" Ethel turned to Livy.

"Yeah," she answered as she sank onto the soda canister.

"This has sure been a heck of a day," Ethel said, looking back across the street.

"You can say that again," Livy agreed.

Mary Ann hung up the phone from speaking to her husband. She then hollered to Ethel and Livy. "Let's call it a day and get out of here before anything else crazy happens."

"Agreed," Ethel yelled back as Livy watched her mother begin locking up the pharmacy. Barbara followed Lucy to the back door to let her out and locked up behind her. Livy heard the big wooden board fall across the door, securing it for the night.

Barbara reappeared and retrieved her purse from the back cash register counter before she and Mary Ann walked to the front.

Ethel turned on the jewelry display case light while Livy switched on the window floods and then ran a rag over the counter one last time. Before she had finished, the phone rang and she picked it up.

"Stephens'" Livy said lamely, letting the fatigue of the day come through.

"Livy?" a husky voice on the other end asked.

"Yeah," she answered.

"Hey, it's Mitch Stapleton."

Livy stopped in mid-wipe and mid-breath.

"Yeah?" she managed.

"Hey, do you want to walk me off the field tonight?" He sounded almost scared to be asking.

"Yeah," she answered.

"Okay, then. I'll see you after the game."

"Yeah," she said, hanging up the phone.

She stood there a moment replaying the conversation.

"Oh my God!" she screamed in her head. *"All I said was 'Yeah.' What a complete and total moron he must think I am. I am such a dork! There is no way he's still gonna want me to walk him off the field. He's probably told everyone what a stupid dumb head I am. He's probably wishing he'd never…"*

The phone rang again and Livy's mind told her not to answer because it was probably Mitch calling back to tell her to forget it because he didn't date imbeciles. But, she mustered her courage and picked it up anyway.

"Stephens' Drug," she droned.

"Woo Hoo!" she heard Stevy scream. "Mitch asked you ouwwut…" she singsonged. "And you said yeeesess," she singsonged again.

"Oh shut up," Livy ordered, pretending it was no big deal.

"What did he say?" Stevy squealed.

"Come on Livy, let's go," Livy heard her mother calling from the front door. "This could not have been a stranger day," she overheard her say to Ethel and Barbara.

"I'll tell you later. I have to go," Livy told Stevy before hanging up. Both Livy and Ethel got their purses before Livy grabbed her jacket, swung it around her shoulder, and sauntered to the front door like the queen she thought she was.

Mary Ann held open the door for all of them.

"Good night girls," she said waving to Ethel and Barbara. "See you, Monday."

"Well see ya," Barbara replied.

"You ready to go home?" Mary Ann asked Livy, "or should we go check on your grandmother?"

"Granny's just fine," Livy reported, knowing she was. "Besides, I have to get ready for the Toilet Bowl."

"Oh yeah, I guess I better get ready to go watch your brothers," Mary Ann agreed as she locked the drugstore door "Let's get going."

Chapter Twenty-Seven

The Prince Isn't Charming

*L*ivy rode with her mother to the game and promptly ditched her to go in search of her friends. Stevy was sitting next to Bebe at the very top of the bleachers. She bounded up them and sat down next to them.

"Heard you're walking the Hunka Hunka off the field." Bebe fluttered her eyelashes and did her famous Marilyn Monroe shoulder roll.

"Shut up." Livy shoved her.

"Well, Miss Cellaneous over here has her own news." Stevy shoved Bebe too.

"What?" Livy's eyes grew wide.

"I'm walking off Jakey." She grinned.

"You are? Really?" Livy returned the grin.

"Yep, he called me right before I left and asked."

Stevy cleared her throat and looked at Bebe, waiting for some acknowledgment. "Oh yeah, Stevy set it up with Brandon."

"Cool! We all have our Prince Charmings!" Livy gloated. "The cheerleaders are going to be so mad that the senior boys are letting freshmen walk them off."

"Who cares?" Stevy waved them off. "They're just jealous."

"Who's jealous?" Livy looked up to see Michael as he was sitting down backward in the row in front of them so that he could face them.

"The high school cheerleaders," Stevy answered.

"We're walking off Jakey and Mitch," Bebe informed him. "Those girls aren't going to like that we are impeding on their territory."

"You're right. They're just jealous," Michael agreed. "Don't worry about it."

The group spent the rest of the game gossiping and scheming, unless Brandon, Jakey, or Mitch's names were announced over the loud speaker for a good play. Then, the girls would swoon, cheer, and fan themselves in hysterical excitement, acting as if the objects of their affections had just been given an Academy Award.

When the game was over, and it was time to walk down to the field, Livy found her face flushing and her heart fluttering. She was sure that Mitch was going to be her husband. In fact, she had already in her mind, named their two children.

They would have one boy and one girl. The boy would come first so that he could protect his little sister. His name would be Mitch too, of course. Their little girl would be Monica, full of sophistication and grace. They would live in New York or London, maybe even Paris – anywhere but Oklahoma. Mitch would be a doctor. She would be a famous reporter. Their lives would be perfect.

"Come with me," she turned to Michael after Stevy and Bebe had already bolted the moment the final buzzer rang.

"Okay." He followed her down the stairs. "Can you believe that it was Lester's wife and daughter who were robbing people?" Michael was still displaying his excitement over the day's outcome.

"We are bona fide heroes," Livy announced as they made their way to the field.

"How so?"

She looked at her friend as if he were crazy. "Um, we helped solve it. Duh."

"Oh yeah!" Michael took a theatrical bow as they arrived at the huddle where the players were listening to the coaches both praise and critique them.

Michael and Livy walked around the outside of the huddle until Livy spotted Mitch. She pointed him out to Michael and smiled.

"Oh, my gawd. She's in looove." Michael pursed his lips as he elongated the word.

Livy rolled her eyes. "Shhh." She admonished her friend. "He's going to hear you."

The coaches droned on, and Livy was sure they would never stop. She saw Stevy and Bebe on the opposite side of the assembled players and waved. Bebe stuck out her tongue.

The coaches finally called for a prayer and the players bowed their heads. Livy again forgot her upbringing, and instead of participating in the prayer, she used the time to ogle her true love.

"Amen," she heard the group echo the coach. Her heart jumped again, realizing she was just seconds away from actually touching the arm of Mitch Stapleton, as she escorted him from the field. She turned to Michael.

"Oh, my God. My hands are dripping. I might as well throw a clam on his arm, it couldn't be any worse than my hands." She tried to wipe them on Michael's shirt.

"Ewww! Stop!" He backed away, looking disgusted.

"Hey, Livy." It was Mitch.

She turned around and everything she had spent the evening planning to say, slipped away. She just stood there and stared at his gorgeous blue eyes and his chiseled face.

"Ready to go?" He looked at her before glaring at Michael. She nodded.

He stuck out his arm for her to take. She did. But then he turned to Michael. "Get lost, fag," he spat.

Livy stopped in her tracks and turned to Mitch. "What did you say?"

"I told your homo friend to get lost."

By that time, Stevy, Brandon, Bebe, and Jakey had made their way over.

Livy looked at her friends, unsure of how to respond. Her knees began to shake. She removed her arm from Mitch's.

"What's the deal?" He looked at her like she was crazy.

"He's not a fag."

"Well, what is he then? Mitch laughed. He looked to his buddies for support. They only looked at the ground. A crowd was beginning to form, including the cheerleaders who were giving the girls dirty looks.

"It's okay, Livy." Michael said, trying to play the situation down. "I'll catch up with you later." He turned to go.

Livy was paralyzed. Stevy and Bebe watched her with caution. The cheerleaders giggled and talked amongst themselves while pointing at her. Everything she had wanted for months was right there in her reach, literally waiting for her to take it. She could be the most popular girl in school or she could be the biggest dork – the very thing she had feared Mitch would think about her just that morning after Old Pete had shoplifted. She felt as if she couldn't breathe. She saw Michael walking away. Mitch grabbed her arm again and started to walk.

As if she were in a dream, Livy stopped and bit her lip.

"You're a dork." She pulled away from the football player. "You're the dork, not me." She shook her head at him in disbelief.

Mitch stared at her as if she had two heads. "Whatever." He shrugged.

"Stupid freshman," Livy overheard the cheerleaders say, and she felt the embarrassment rise from her feet to her head.

In a split second, a tall brunette cheerleader grabbed Mitch's arm and pulled him away.

Mitch turned to his buddies. "Come on guys."

Brandon and Jakey looked at each other a moment before Jakey answered. "We'll catch up with you later." Mitch opened his mouth to say something, but then thought better of it. "Whatever," he repeated.

Pogo came bouncing up and told the remaining group they should all hit the Eater Upper for burgers and shakes. Everyone agreed.

"Want to come Livy?" Stevy asked her.

"Naw, I think I'll hang out with Michael."

"He can come too," Brandon said.

Livy smiled at him, happy in the knowledge that not all the popular boys were like Mitch.

"Thanks Brandon, but I think I'll just lay low tonight."

"Hey Michael, wait up." She turned to follow him. "I'll see you guys later," she told Stevy and Bebe over her shoulder, then she turned back around just before the hot tears sprang from her eyes.

She caught up with Michael and they walked a few moments in silence before he half whispered, "You didn't have to do that. I'm used to it by now."

"Yeah, I did." She wiped her eyes with her fingertips. "You're one of my best friends."

The two continued to walk in silence. When they got to the main gate, Livy saw her mother. "Can I go to Michael's and play some pool for a while?"

Her mother looked at her watch. "I'll pick you up at 10:00."

Livy nodded and took Michael's arm in hers. They began to walk to his house. She smiled at him. "You can be my Prince Charming."

"Honey," he said, tilting his head. "I'm no Prince Charming. Now, Queen Bee? That I can wrap myself around," he laughed.

Livy laughed too.

Final Chapter

The Greatest Lesson

*L*ivy returned at the age of forty to the small and forever sacred town of her youth. She stood at the end of the street looking at all that remained of the place.

The drugstore had long ago closed, locking up for the last time a year before she left for college. Although she remembered their home telephone ringing in the wee hours of the night, and her mother leaving her bed to fill emergency prescriptions, there had been no loyalty when new and improved came to town.

Mr. Pendleton decided that Main Street was no longer the place to house his grocery. He built another store, complete with a brand-new pharmacy, next to the medical center on the west side of town. It was only a matter of a few months before the traffic at Stephens' Drug had completely vanished, leaving everything to be auctioned off, and Mary Ann to go to work for a big chain pharmacy in Maiden.

Most of the other stores Livy frequented when she was young, had also taken their leave. The town was now only a shell of its former self, with less than a dozen stores remaining on the once populated street.

Livy remembered when she couldn't wait to leave this place – this town of oddballs, misfits, and just ordinary folks. But, as she wandered down the street where she came of age, where she began to develop the dreams she had for her life, she could see her foolishness in wanting to leave.

Lucy was right when she predicted Livy would someday miss the place. And also, as predicted, she and several of the people who helped shape Livy's life were gone. Alberta, Old Pete, two of the morning coffee gang, John Davis and Festus Marney, had passed on. They were joined by Ms. Fran, the tag agent; Bengal Billy, the boxer; Bob Cutter; and Mr. Walter, the principal. Livy's grandfather and both grandmothers were gone as well.

Livy had yearned for something bigger, better, and more exciting. She wanted the thrill of the big city – the glamor and fame. Her wish came true. She left after high school and went to college to become a broadcast journalist. She became a television news reporter, living and working in some of the largest cities in the country. She also covered some of the biggest stories in recent history.

She searched the world for interesting people and met presidents, philanthropists, CEOs of Fortune 500 Companies, and other world leaders, but none – not one – could compare to the people she had known from home.

The beautiful thing she found in those people, that she was never able to find again, was that they were never afraid to be themselves, flaws and all. They were happy to be just what the good Lord made them.

It was all the people who were gone, and some who were still living, that taught her that this was a place like no other. The town was all that was the best of her.

It was the place she learned to care for those who were different. It allowed her to see beyond their façade, and into their deepest desires, hopes and dreams. It taught her the value of every human spirit – that they *are* spirits, and not black, white, Native American, gay or straight.

It made her a better journalist because she learned to respect other's vulnerabilities. It made her a better human being, because it enlightened her that everyone is flawed, and real perfection only comes from being able to forgive each other for those flaws and cherish each other for them too. She came to understand that it was her own flaws which taught her to rely on others and her God.

Livy's hometown was a place where people took care of one another – where the lowliest were also the loveliest. It was a place where both a local and a stranger could find solace. It was Shiloh, a place of peace and rest.

When Livy needed to bring herself back to wholeness, it was to this wonderful, crazy, and utterly unique place she would journey – if only in her mind.

If she could have given her own daughter any precious and everlasting gift, it would be to have been raised in this place, instead of the city. Konawa was the place she called home.

As she stared down the street, reliving all that had molded her, she imagined that one day she would lay alongside her grandmother, grandfather and other relatives and friends on the hill where they were all put to rest.

From there she would watch the going-ons in this extra ordinary place, and she would quietly chuckle to herself as she remembered the lessons she learned from the people who came into the drugstore.

Acknowledgments

I want to thank my biggest supporters, my husband, Douglas, and my daughter, Brealyn Elizabeth Wren, who sat through countless readings of the manuscript. Brealyn is also the creative mind behind the book's cover.

I want to thank my incredible (and talented) step-son, Oliver W. Shelton for his invaluable advice regarding the direction of this series.

To my hometown friend, and fellow author, Al Gattenby, many thanks for all your advice about the publication of this book and even more for the recommendation of our mutual, and amazing editor, Stuart Blandford.

To Stuart, first, I love that you are Southern and understand the Southern voice. Secondly, I love that because you have thirteen and fifteen-year-old daughters, you knew how to fully appreciate the teen girl drama of Livy.

Finally, to the many friends and family members who have continued to encourage me to never stop writing, I promise, I won't.

About The Author

S tacy D. Shelton, or "SD" as her friends know her, is a multi-award-winning former broadcast and print journalist. She loves everything Southern, including gardening, college football, visiting with neighbors on the front porch, and fried okra.

She resides in Oklahoma with her husband, Doug, and their three dogs, Teddy; and Walter and Harvey (who were born in Konawa and have their own Facebook following under #BiteyBabies).

She loves to travel, explore abandoned houses, and see what's down any overgrown dirt road. But mostly, she loves to write. *The Drugstore* is the first book in an eight part series, so watch for the next installment, *The Life of Old Pete,* coming soon.

Connect with SD on Facebook at facebook.com/sd.sheltonauthor